Olivia's Story

Cheryl OBrien

Copyright © 2014 Cheryl OBrien

All rights reserved.

ISBN 10: 1500326801
ISBN-13: 978-1500326807

DEDICATION

In this life, you have met people who inspired you to hope - to look beyond what was or is in front of you and into the future you had hoped for. Remember their words of encouragement. Hold on to the memory of their hugs. Look back for a moment and see them behind you smiling and believing you could do it. Honor them by moving forward and trying once again because they believed in you. That goal that brings happiness is so close to achieving. Don't give up now.

Jeremiah 29:11

For I know the plans I have for you declares the Lord

Plans for good and not for evil

Plans for hope and a future

Chapter One

"Charles, how is your father?" Aunt Lucille asked as we sat at her table.

I watched my brother look up at her from his meal. He had a family affection for Aunt Lucille. She had always been kind to my three brothers and me. Charles was the eldest of us. Although my mother had passed, he felt responsible to represent both my parents by his good behavior when we were among people of influence.

"Quite well, Aunt Lucille. I'm sure Father regrets that he could not be here. We are delighted that you have included us in your invitations." Charles replied.

"How could I not? You four are the only children of my dear departed sister. God, rest her soul. Not to mention," she whispered to me, "the only interesting people here."

I giggled and got a stern look from Charles. I wanted to give him a sassy look back for his scolding glare, but I thought better of it.

"Jacob, pass your sister a glass of wine." Uncle Peter insisted.

"Uncle Peter, I fear that my father would not approve of Olivia having a glass of wine. He is insistent on keeping her from indulging in things he believes are beyond her years." My brother Keith told him.

"Even as she is almost eighteen?" Uncle Peter was surprised by the restriction.

"She is his precious jewel, Uncle Peter. All of us have been sworn to protect her innocence." My brother Charles told him.

I was almost embarrassed as he said it.

My aunt patted my hand. "It is as it should be Olivia. Fathers are always aware of their daughters."

"Yes, it seems the case with me. I have four guardians over my life. Someone is always watching over me." I told her.

"I understand your frustration, but you are a beauty. They have reason to protect you." My aunt tried to soften the atmosphere.

When supper was finished we left the table with the others. Many men and women filled the sitting room and the outdoor balcony of my uncle's home. My brothers chose who would be first on watch over my life. Keith was selected first for the duty. As I walked out to the balcony a young man tried to approach me. Keith motioned for him to move along.

"Keith, please don't embarrass me. It is merely a conversation he wants to enjoy with me. I will die a spinster if you and the others don't give me a chance to meet anyone." I told him.

"His station in life is lower than ours. Father would not approve of him. I do not want him to entertain the idea that you are approachable." Keith told me.

"Am I to be confined to boring female conversation all my life?" I complained. "You and Jacob share adventures and Charles surrounds himself with friends, male and female. Do you know how lonely it is being me with these types of restrictions?" I asked him.

"Olivia, we are aware of the restrictions Father has placed on your life. You are his only daughter and the youngest of us. If there be a curse, maybe that is one. I'm sorry, but if I gave you the freedom you desire, Father would take a whip to my back." Keith said.

"Babysitting again, Keith?" His friend Robert asked as he came to join us.

That really hurt my feelings. It was all I could do not to cry. Charles saw the expression on my face. He excused himself from those enjoying his company and came to me. "Keith, take a walk with your friend."

Keith walked away with Robert to join the other girls who were not so watched over as I was.

"What did he say?" Charles whispered.

"Charles, can we leave? Everyone here is so used to your protection of me that no one dares to approach me for even a minute. Keith's friend called it babysitting. I am humiliated and hurt by all this isolation."

He watched the tears fall from my eyes as I spoke.

"I hate to see you upset, Olivia. It breaks my heart." He

said. "Robert is just frustrated that Keith won't let him near you. The comment was surely meant to upset Keith more than you." He said.

"I do not want Robert near me. He is ill-mannered and insensitive." I told him. "If you want to protect me from someone, protect me from him."

"I heard the last girl he dated had a wart right on the tip of her nose." Charles joked.

I laughed. "And a broom, no doubt."

"There's my girl. Be patient with us, Olivia. We all adore you. We just want the best for you." Charles said.

We talked for an hour. Charles could keep me laughing. He was very entertaining. I always understood why people gravitated toward him.

"I have seen a vision on the balcony standing next to Charles Douglas. She is beautiful." Paul declared as he arrived late to join his father.

"That is his sister, Olivia. Turn away son. That family has her under lock and key. Each of her brothers stands watch over her. Her father has never let a boy or a man near her. He guards her virtue like a priceless treasure. She is well-educated and bred for the best connection her father can find." Mr. Stephens told him.

"She is the treasure I've been looking for. It is a pity I have to deal with a guardian over her life." Paul replied. "I could easily be in love with her."

"Each young man in this room could easily be in love with her, but her brothers will not allow it." Mr. Stephens told him.

"Then it is time we stepped forward so you can introduce me, Father." Paul suggested.

Mr. Stephens smiled. "A polite introduction might get you a smile. Come with me."

They walked toward us unnoticed which was to their benefit.

"Charles Douglas." Mr. Stephens interrupted us.

"Yes, Mr. Stephens." Charles turned around.

"I would like to introduce you to my youngest son Paul. He has returned from a recent stay in France and is familiar with your father's business. I thought that since you and he were about the same age, you might have some things in common. Paul is trying to reconnect to this area. He hasn't met many people yet. Your uncle's dinner party seemed a good opportunity to do that." Mr. Stephens said.

Charles extended his hand politely and shook Paul's. "It is nice to meet you. This is my dear sister Olivia." Charles introduced me.

Paul took my hand politely and kissed the back of it. "So nice to meet you, Miss Olivia." He smiled at me.

I smiled at him. "It is very nice to meet you, Paul."

Charles felt sympathy for my loneliness. It caused him to stay by my side and carry on a short conversation with Paul. "Why were you in France?" Charles asked him.

"I have relatives there. They allowed me to visit for an extended time. I was learning about the wine business literally from the ground up. It is a fascinating industry. I understand your father is a major importer of French wine for this area. He was listed as one of my future connections. I've been hired to sell the family wine in this area." Paul explained.

"Were you constantly busy with the wine business?" Charles asked.

"I had some free time. France is an amazing country. There are plenty of things to do and to see. I enjoy physical sports. I've always been interested in those things that challenge my physical and intellectual limitations. Anything worth doing is worth doing well." Paul said.

"How are you on a horse?" Charles asked him.

"Very comfortable. What did you have in mind?" He asked.

"We are a man short on the polo field tomorrow morning. Would you be interested in joining our team? I had thought we might have to withdraw. If you are up to it, the games start at nine in the morning." Charles told him.

"I am honored you would consider me. I certainly would like to join your team. Where is the event?" Paul asked.

"Stanfield Meadows. I'm sure your father is familiar with the area." Charles said.

"Will you be there to cheer for your brother's team, Miss Olivia?" Paul asked.

"I should like to be, but I'm not sure I will be able." I

answered.

"It would be an honor to have your presence at the games. It was very nice meeting you both. I look forward to tomorrow's game." Paul said. "Excuse us please. I'm sure my mother must be looking for us."

Charles and I watched him walk away.

"What do you think of him, Charles?" I asked him.

"I think he is a liar." Charles replied.

"What would make you believe that?" I asked him. "He seemed very informative and confident."

"His manner is suspect. I noticed a slight French accent in his tone. Some of the things he spoke about may be true, but I know fluff when I hear it. He was trying to impress you with the line about pushing his physical and mental limitations. I just don't buy the package." Charles told me.

"He admitted he has stayed in France for a long time. People pick up accents when they are around the people who speak like that enough. Will you let me come to watch the game tomorrow?" I asked him.

"Yes, but only because I want you to watch him fail. I don't trust that he even knows how to play the game. I wonder if he has ever been on a horse." Charles said.

"Why would you accept him on your team?" I asked him.

"I hate to withdraw and I like a good laugh. It is only a game." Charles said as Jacob came to me to relieve him.

"Ah, the next brother to watch over me." I complained.

Charles kissed me on the cheek. "Olivia, it's in the rule book. You might as well relax about it. Our guardianship will not change too quickly." He walked away.

"Paul, why would you agree to play on their team? You've never played polo before."

"Dear Father, I ride quite well. Just explain the rules to me. I know I can manage." Paul said. "Besides, I never did tell him that I knew the game. I just told him that I was comfortable on a horse and we are both sure of that. Certainly someone you know has the equipment for such a sport."

"This seems a great adventure to you." His father smiled.

"I plan on impressing Miss Olivia and her brother." Paul said. "Let us find my beautiful mother so she can introduce me to our hosts for the evening."

The party broke up at ten o'clock. I rode home with Jacob and Keith. Charles went to his own home. He promised to come in the morning to get me before the games began. Keith and Jacob had plans and father was away on business. I knew my Aunt Lucille and Uncle Peter would be there to keep me company.

The next morning Charles was at the house at eight o'clock. We arrived at the Stanfield Meadows about fifteen minutes later. Charles was surprised to see Paul on the field practicing shots. He waved him over.

Paul rode up to us on his horse. "Good morning, Miss Olivia. Good morning, Charles." He smiled.

"How long have you been here?" Charles asked.

"Since seven." He answered.

"Why so early?" Charles asked.

"I've never played the game before. My father explained it and I contacted a cousin who had some equipment. I figured if I was going to help you win, I should give it my best. So I've been at it since seven." Paul explained.

"I thought you had played before." Charles said.

"No. I only told you I was comfortable on a horse and I am. Polo seemed a new challenge. I like to learn new things, so I said yes." He explained as he got down from his horse.

"You look beautiful today, Miss Olivia. I hope you enjoy the game. If I mess up, please feel free to laugh at me." Paul was very friendly.

"I should enjoy that if it happens. It would be better though if you did not. Charles enjoys winning." I told him.

"Well, who wouldn't?" He smiled. "Charles, when do I meet the rest of the team?"

"The other two are Leonard Dobbs and Darnell Fernie. You should get along fine. I brought you a shirt." Charles handed it to him.

"Excuse me while I change. I'll meet you back here." He walked off with his horse.

"You were wrong about him Charles." I was delighted about that.

"I may have been. It's just hard to believe all his charm." Charles remained cautious.

"He is just friendly and easy to talk to." I defended him.

"Keep your distance Olivia. He is not a potential suitor for you." Charles reminded me.

"Charles, why couldn't he just be a friend?" I asked him.

"He's a man and you are a young lady, that's why." He answered.

"Really, Charles, women have male friends." I insisted.

"It won't happen, Olivia. If he is around, I will be too." Charles insisted.

We spotted my aunt and uncle making their way toward us. Aunt Lucille kissed my cheek when she got close to me. I really loved her. She was such fun. She took me by the hand while Uncle Peter spoke with Charles. We walked toward the seating area.

"So tell me, Olivia, do any of these men strike a heart cord with you?" She whispered.

"Yes, actually." I whispered back.

"Oh, do tell me. I love keeping our little secrets from your father and your brothers." She whispered.

"Paul Stephens is the new man on my brother's team. He is very handsome and quite friendly." I told her.

"I shall look for him." My aunt said.

We giggled together as we found a seat. Then we watched for him as Charles' team took their positions.

"Oh my! Yes, Olivia. You have extraordinary taste." She said as she caught sight of him.

"Taste in what?" My uncle asked as he sat down.

"Well, that horse, of course." Aunt Lucille pointed at the horse Darnell Fernie was riding. "Magnificent, just magnificent."

I tried my best not to laugh. I had to turn away from her.

We watched the game and cheered for the team. "Come on, Olivia, let's get a closer look." She dragged me out of my seat and we walked to the front of the crowd together. My uncle stayed behind.

"Aunty, you are such fun." I told her.

"I know. I'm a twenty-year-old woman stuck in a forty-year-old body. Thank goodness your uncle is nearly blind. He still thinks I'm beautiful." She joked.

"He sees very well." I laughed.

Paul spotted me at the front of the crowd with my aunt. He winked at me as he rode by. I was grateful Charles didn't see it.

"He likes you too, Olivia." My aunt whispered.

"My father and brothers won't let him get near me." I told her.

"He's very clever. He has already seen you and spoken to

you twice. He will find a way to touch your heart. Give him time; and for goodness sake, don't give him away. Once your father and brothers know you are interested in him, the walls will go up." She warned me.

"I don't know how I would have survived them if it were not for your care and friendship." I told her.

"Don't you worry, my dear. I will always be available to you." She assured me.

Paul made sure to score a goal. My brother had to admit he was an asset to the team. He rode his horse quite well. His parents were able to catch the last part of the game. His father made sure to introduce me to his mother, Mrs. Stephens. She was very nice. They stood next to us and cheered for their son and his team. I had no idea Paul had set that up with his father so that he could have more of a conversation with me in their presence after the game.

My aunt and uncle were getting along very well with his parents. My aunt wanted them to stay nearby. She saw the plan unfolding. Paul and Charles joined us after the game. Mr. Stephens spoke with Charles and my uncle to distract him. My aunt spoke with Mrs. Stephens. It gave Paul a few minutes to speak with me. He offered to get me a drink. We took advantage of Charles being distracted as we walked away from the table together. It was only a short walk, still in view of Charles if he chose to look.

"Olivia, I know the routine your brothers have about protecting you from the likes of me. I want you to know I am a patient and persistent man. You're beautiful. I would spend lots of time explaining this, but I know Charles will be right over when he realizes we are talking to each other. I want to get to know you better, Olivia. Is that alright with you?" He asked me.

"Yes, but I don't know how it will be possible. Charles and my brothers have been sheltering me for years." I told him.

"Leave it to me. Just be patient. I'll find a way to spend time with you. I guarantee it." He smiled and handed me my drink and another. "Here, this is for your aunt. I have one for my mother."

"You are clever." I told him.

"Yes, I am." He said confidently as we walked back to the table. "Here, Mother, your drink." Paul handed it to her.

"Thank you." She replied as she took it.

"Here, Aunty, Paul got a drink for you too." I handed her the drink.

"Thank you, Paul." She said.

"My pleasure, Mrs. Winters." Paul said. "I know how it is when my father distracts the men with his pursuit of sports rules and such. They can get their own drinks." He went over to join their conversation. "Let's not be rude to the ladies. There are more games coming up. Get yourselves a drink and let's have a pleasant morning in their company."

"Well said." My uncle agreed.

"Olivia and I need to go." Charles told them as he put his hand on the back of my chair.

"Oh, Charles, let her stay with us. She is enjoying the weather and the games. I wanted Olivia to come back with me to my house. We are working on a dress together. It would save you and your brothers a trip if we took her directly from here." My aunt tried to persuade him.

"We would be happy to drop her off at the house later." Uncle Peter said. "Your Aunt Lucille loves to spend time with Olivia."

He watched as Paul continued to talk to his father away from the table. He seemed to be interested in studying the game and not Olivia. Charles hesitated as he thought about it. He knew Jacob and Keith had plans.

"Alright, but she needs to be back by four o'clock. Father arrives home at five. He will be upset with me if she is not there." Charles' tone was serious.

"Thank you, Charles. I promise she will be back by four." My aunt told him as she squeezed my hand under the table.

Charles got Paul's attention and waved him over.

"Here it comes." He said to his father as he left him. He walked back to Charles. "Yes?"

"Paul, can I talk to you for a minute?" Charles asked.

"Oh, no, Aunty, he wouldn't." I whispered and put my head down in embarrassment.

"Look up, Olivia. You are not responsible for this conversation." My aunt whispered.

I put my head up and watched Paul.

Olivia's Story

"Sure." Paul put down his drink and winked and smiled at me while his back was turned toward my brother.

I made sure not to react. My aunt saw it too and she didn't respond to it either. She was keeping our secret.

"Good game today." Paul said.

"Yes, it was. Paul, about my sister." Charles started.

"Yes, she's a precious child isn't she? I'm surprised she didn't want to bring any of her friends with her to see you play. She speaks highly of you. That is a delight coming from so young a sister." Paul said. "If you are worried that she will annoy me, don't be. She is more endearing than many of my younger cousins."

"Well, good then." Charles was surprised by his comments. "I'll be in touch."

"If you need an extra man again, let me know. I had a really good time." Paul said as Charles left.

Charles didn't trust him. He stayed in the shadows for fifteen minutes watching Paul to see where he would be focusing his attention. He watched as Paul took his father to the front of the crowd to watch the game closely. Paul was pointing out things to his father and they were both cheering for the players. Paul knew Charles didn't trust him. He didn't come near me for thirty minutes. Charles had left by then.

Then he sat down next to me. We talked casually with all the others at our table. It was so nice to finally be in the company of a man, especially one who had so many interesting stories. He was very careful not to give the impression that I was his focus. He included everyone at the table. When my uncle walked away with his father, he took my hand under the table and held it in his.

"Paul, would you mind getting Mrs. Winters and me another drink?" His mother asked him.

"Of course. It would be my pleasure. Olivia, could you help me carry the drinks?" He asked.

"Yes, of course." I got up with him.

"Paul, that refreshment stand is empty. I think you might want to try the one further away." My aunt suggested.

"Alright." He agreed.

He talked to me as we walked together. "Just in case you are wondering, I told your brother that I thought of you as a precious child. I promised him that I wouldn't be annoyed with your behavior. I also told him that we talked about him and your great opinion of him. I think he was thoroughly surprised. Of course, I don't think of you as a child. Some day, when I gain more of the family trust, I will tell that to all of them. Your aunt seems to be helping us." He said as he looked back at her.

"My aunt hasn't really approved of the overprotective behavior of my father and my brothers. She is trying to make my life better. They have been so strict that I am restricted from female company too, especially if my friends have older brothers." I told him.

"Sounds like a very lonely life." He said.

"It has been." I admitted.

"I want to change that for you." Paul said.

"I know. I'm enjoying today very much. You are so friendly. You must have many friends." I said.

"Yes, I do. Most of them are in France, although I seem to be gaining friends here. I haven't been here to visit the area since my parents moved here a few years ago." He told me.

"Do you plan on going back to France?" I asked him.

"Eventually, but not right away. I have to settle in this area for a while and build up a demand for the wine my family sells from France." He told me.

"I hope you are successful." I told him as we stood in front of the refreshment stand.

"I always have some degree of success in all things. I'm guessing you are eighteen. Am I correct?" He asked.

I smiled. "No, you are not. A lady should not reveal her age, but I don't agree with that philosophy entirely. I am seventeen."

"Oh, so you are a child." He teased and saw the hurt in my manner. "I'm very sorry, Olivia. I was just teasing. I didn't mean it."

"We should go back." I took my aunt's drink with mine.

"Olivia, please understand my nature. I thought my comment would amuse you. I never meant it to hurt your feelings or to insult you. Honestly." He spoke as we walked back to the table. "Please, Olivia, stop walking for a moment and look at me. I beg of you." He said as he stepped in front of

me.

"You give me little choice." I told him as I stopped.

"Olivia, you are a vision to me. I've never seen or met anyone as sweet and beautiful as you are. I would never desire to intentionally hurt your feelings or insult you. Please let me take those words back. You are a beautiful woman. I don't consider you a child at all. Please give me a chance to step back into your good grace." He apologized.

I smiled at him. "That was a very nice apology. I would bet that you've had plenty of practice."

"Did you just put me in my place?" He was astonished with my strategy.

"Just drawing a line in the sand, Mr. Stephens."

"You look at me that way and I can't help but notice that you have the most incredible eyes. They will soon capture my soul." He said.

"You, Sir, are a poet. I should be careful around you. Your words are dangerous to my heart." I told him.

"That is because I speak the truth and you know it." He said. "Let's get back to the table. I must spend time with your uncle away from you or he will become suspicious of my intentions toward you."

"You know best." I walked with him back to the table.

He spent time with my uncle watching some more of the matches. My uncle introduced him to a few people. I tried not to watch him. I noticed he had met a few of the young women standing near the front of the crowd. I noticed he was very charming to them. They seemed to enjoy his company.

"He has a way about him, doesn't he?" My aunt whispered.

"Maybe Charles is right. Maybe he can't be trusted." I whispered back.

Mrs. Stephens leaned toward me. "I know I am not supposed to be in on this, but my husband spoke to me before we came. Olivia, my son is quite taken with you. I can see it in his eyes. This social show is just that. Don't doubt him, Olivia. He is sincerely interested in you. This is just strategy. I promise."

I was surprised by what she said.

"Watch him, Olivia. He will come back to you and find a way to let you know." She told me.

I watched him. When he turned around he made sure no one was looking. Then he scrunched up his face and made crazy eyes. He pointed in the direction of the other women.

I laughed and he smiled.

He pointed at me and then put his hand over his heart. He came back to the table. "I'm sorry, but I have to leave. It has been a pleasure to be in such grand company." He said to us.

"It was very nice meeting you again, Paul." My aunt said.

"Goodbye, Sweetheart, your father and I will see you at home." His mother kissed him on the cheek as he leaned down beside her.

My uncle and his father were still at the front of the crowd as he left.

"Oh, Olivia. I forgot to give him the house keys. Please hurry to catch up with him before he leaves." She handed me the keys.

I knew it was a set up. I took them and went after him. He was waiting behind one of the large trees. He caught me as I was about to pass by him and pulled me toward him.

"Your keys Mr. Stephens." I held them up.

"I would like nothing more than to kiss you right here, but I don't want our first kiss to be rushed. I will see you again, Olivia. You can count on that. Those other girls meant nothing. It was just strategy. I hope you realize that." He said sincerely.

"I do." I told him.

He kissed me on the cheek. "I hope you don't mind. I know I should have asked first, but I was honestly afraid you would deny me. Please go back now before you are missed."

My aunt and I had a marvelous afternoon. She made sure that I was home at four o'clock. Father came in at five sharp. His first moment was spent finding me.

"Olivia!" He greeted me with a hug.

I hugged him back. "I've missed you, Father. Did you have a good trip?"

"Yes. How was your aunt's party?" He asked me as he removed his jacket.

"Boring. Father, when are you going to let people get near me? My reputation as the protected daughter has driven even other women away from me. I find the only people I can talk to are you and my brothers, and Aunty, of course. Father, please let me have some freedom. Charles, Keith, and Jacob stand over me like protective dogs." I complained.

He was frustrated with me. "It is for your own good, Olivia. You are beautiful and sweet. Many are aware that we are a family of some means. I just don't want anyone to take advantage of your innocence. It is a father's duty to protect his daughter."

"Father, please loosen the chains a little. Have my brothers stand at the other end of the room. Allow me the opportunity to talk with people alone, to have my own conversations. Allow me to dance with a partner I am not related to. Please, Father. I'm not asking you to let me outside alone with a man somewhere on the street. I'm just asking to have the same opportunities to develop socially as other girls my age. I'm lonely. You know I am lonely." I pleaded with him.

"Alright, Olivia. I will trust you not to encourage the wrong kind of attention. I will speak to your brothers and tell them to watch you from across the room. You may have your own conversations and dance partners who are not related to you." He agreed.

I kissed him on the cheek and hugged him. "Thank you Father."

Chapter Two

"There is a young man by the name of Paul Stephens to see you, Sir Douglas." Our butler announced to my father.

"That is the young man I told you about, Father. He was quite impressive on the polo field. He is the youngest son of your friend, Mr. Trevor Stephens." Charles explained.

"Send him in, James." My father told the butler.

When Paul entered the room, Charles shook his hand immediately. "Nice to see you again, Paul."

"Thank you, Charles." Paul smiled.

My father got up from his chair. "You are Trevor's son?"

"Yes, Sir Douglas. My father sends his regards." Paul waited for my father to extend his hand, but he didn't.

"State your business, Mr. Stephens." My father stood facing him.

"Sir Douglas, I understand that you have secured the largest import business of high priced wines for this area and the marketing of those wines." Paul said.

"That would be correct." My father replied.

"I am in contact with the producers of Chalon Wine. It is an extraordinary wine produced in the finest vineyard in France. I brought two bottles for your sampling. Once you have tasted the contents, I am sure you will agree that its amazing qualities match or exceed the brands that you are currently importing. The best feature of this wine is that it is not as expensive as the majority of the wines sold today. The owners of this fine wine would like to go through you to import the wine into this area." Paul said.

"Years ago I knew the owner of the Chalon Vineyards. His name was Luc Chalon. Are you related to him?" Sir Douglas asked.

"He sold the vineyard at a good price years ago and moved away to a better climate. I heard he was ill at the time. Relatives of mine bought the property. This wine is their creation and God's of course. They just kept the name. Andre Chalon is employed by them as an occasional consultant, but he is not involved in the everyday procedures." Paul explained.

"Charles, have James bring us six glasses to taste this extraordinary wine." My father ordered.

Charles left the room and returned a moment later. They did not have to wait long for James to bring the glasses.

My father poured wine into three of the glasses. Then he picked his up and tipped the glass to check the color of the red wine. "I know Charles only cares about the taste as most wine drinkers do, but if I am going to market this item I need to know what I am agreeing to sell. There are concerns. Is it maroon or possibly ruby in color? Each wine holds its own degree of color." He said as he looked closely at it. "Also, is it watery or dark, dull or brilliant, cloudy or clear? You see wine is like a person. It has facets, personality, and character. If you fail to look closely you cannot fully appreciate the treasure or dismiss the trash you have in front of you."

Paul and Charles held their glasses without tasting the wine until my father had finished his examination.

"After you look, you must smell the wine." He swirled his glass for ten seconds and then took a quick whiff of it to gain the first impression of the aroma of the wine. Then he stuck his nose deep into the glass and inhaled deeply. He swirled the wine again and let the aroma mingle; then he sniffed it again.

Paul and Charles watched the interesting examination waiting for his opinion.

"Gentlemen, so far I am not disappointed in the quality of this wine. Let's see if the taste of it satisfies or disappoints." He took a small sip and let it roll around in his mouth. Then he smiled and swallowed it. "Well done. Very well done." He continued to drink the wine.

Paul and Charles joined him.

"Father, you go through all of that and I can tell at the first taste that I like the wine." Charles said. "It seems a waste of time to go through all that formality."

Paul smiled.

"Do you believe I wasted my time, Mr. Stephens?" My father asked him.

"No, Sir Douglas. I spent a large amount of time doing

exactly what you did so that I could get to know the wine I was promoting. I had to believe in the product before I could present it to you." Paul said.

"What did you learn on a personal level?" My father asked him.

"To look deeper when you find something rare and beautiful." He answered.

At that my father decided that he liked Paul. He extended his hand. "It is a fine wine, Paul. Tell the people you represent that I would very much like to import and market the red wine."

"And the white wine, Sir Douglas?" Paul asked.

"Ah, I have not tasted that yet. Let me savor this one first. I will give you my answer on the white wine tomorrow at this time." My father told him.

"Thank you, Sir Douglas. I will return for your answer tomorrow at this time." Paul said.

"Thank you for coming." My father said. "Charles will walk you to the door."

"Sir Douglas, before I leave my parents wanted me to convey a personal invitation to you and your family. My father is inviting a gathering of friends and acquaintances to celebrate the anniversary of his marriage to my mother. He wishes no gifts, just the pleasure of your company. There will be an over abundance of food as well as music to enjoy. My mother is quite thrilled to be arranging the specifics. She has reminded my father that he shall be dancing with her." Paul told him.

"We would be honored to attend if our schedules permit it. What date is this gathering to be held?" My father asked him.

Paul reached into the inside pocket of his jacket and pulled out an elegantly hand written invitation. "Every detail you will need is in this invitation. However, I will tell you that it is one month from tomorrow on the fourth of June. I expect we will be up quite late." Paul told him. "It is a formal affair."

My father went around to his chair and checked the schedule on his desk. "I will be out of town that day, but I will be sure to send my sons and my daughter to attend the celebration. If I can manage to cancel my appointments, I will be there too. Please tell your father that I will send him notice if my plans can be changed. For now, let him know that Charles, Keith, Jacob and Olivia will be attending."

"Sir Douglas, if any one, including yourself wishes to invite a guest, you are all welcome to do so. My mother merely needs a note of it. She would be overjoyed to add more people to her guest list. She expects quite a good turnout. I would imagine she will keep me busy most of the evening." Paul said.

"We appreciate the personal invitation. I have marked the date down on my calendar. Charles will escort you to the door. It was a pleasure meeting you. I look forward to our meeting tomorrow." My father said. Then he sat down at his desk as Paul left with Charles.

"It should be an interesting evening." Charles remarked.

"If my mother has her way, it will be." Paul told him.

"My father has loosened the chains on Olivia." Charles

informed him.

"I don't understand. What chains?" Paul asked.

"You were not aware that my father has had us guarding Olivia to keep the men away from her?" Charles inquired.

"My father mentioned you were a bit protective of her. I suppose if I had a younger sister, my parents would expect the same thing from me. Referring to her as being chained seems a little more serious than I thought it was. After all, she was enjoying her time at the polo game. She didn't seem weary of your protection. She speaks well of you." Paul told him.

"We've been ordered to watch her from a distance. She has been placed on the honor system. One mistake and my father will have us standing over her again." Charles told him.

"Let me know how that works out for you. If I can help in any way, just let me know. I made a few connections at the polo game including a Miss Sarah Perkins and her friend Amanda Childs. Do you know them?" Paul asked.

"Yes, I know Sarah. She's very attractive and quite available." Charles told him.

"Charles, do you have a crush on her? If you do, I'll back away." Paul offered.

"Actually yes. I was thinking of inviting her to the party." Charles told him.

"Enough said. You go right ahead. There are lots of available women in this area close to our own age. I'm sure Sarah will enjoy your attention that evening more than she would mine. I would be surprised if my mother didn't keep me busy all night." Paul told him.

"I won't see you tomorrow. I'm busy most of this month. I will see you the night of your mother's party. Good luck with the white wine." Charles told him.

"It will sell itself. I'm not worried. Goodbye, Charles." Paul left happy.

Chapter Three

The evening of the Stephens' anniversary party arrived. Charles arranged to escort Sarah Perkins to the party and left Keith and Jacob to make sure I got there. Keith had arranged a date for himself with Danielle Clemons and Jacob had arranged a date for himself with Lauren Masters. They exchanged this information with each other as I was getting ready. There was a big disagreement as to who was going to take me along as a third party.

"How could you not tell me you had arranged a date?" Keith asked him. "I've already made arrangements to pick up Danielle alone. I can't take Olivia with me. I'm trying to make an impression on this girl."

"Well brother we are in the same boat. Father will be furious with us if we don't watch over Olivia. I thought you were free or I wouldn't have arranged to take Lauren. I can't back out of the date now. She'll never speak to me again." Jacob complained.

I heard them arguing over me. I went downstairs. "Brothers, take your dates to the celebration. I will save you the trouble of watching me. I will simply stay home."

"Olivia, you look so lovely and you worked so hard on that

dress. I know you want to go." Keith said.

"It's fine. There will be other celebrations. Go now. Pick up your dates. You've sacrificed enough for me over the years. I can make this one small sacrifice for you." I insisted.

They went but argued all the way out the door. When they arrived with their dates, Charles asked where I was. They admitted the truth to him. He was very angry with both of them.

Paul overheard the argument and interrupted. "Charles, is there a problem I can help you with?"

"My brothers sacrificed our dear sister's evening for the sake of their dates. Olivia is home dressed with no escort and none of us can leave the women we've brought because our first impression will go to hell." Charles complained.

"I think your problem has just been solved." Paul pointed to me as I entered the house.

Charles was more upset as were my other two brothers.

Paul stopped them. "Really, the first sign of independent thinking and you are all ready to jump on her. Look at her. She is an innocent child wanting to enjoy the night. Give her the freedom she requested. Be kind to her. She saved your evening by her sacrifice and ingenuity."

They settled down at his words.

"None of us has the freedom to watch her." Keith reminded his brothers.

"My mother doesn't need me as I thought she would. I

have no woman to focus my attention on this early in the evening and your sister is young, but cheerful. Let me do you this favor and watch over her. If for any reason I spot someone more interesting I will let you know. Then you can work it out among yourselves." Paul offered.

"Are you sure you are not in this to get closer to Olivia?" Jacob asked.

"I remind you that I am much older than your sister. If you are not comfortable with the arrangement, I will just go mingle with the other available women who are closer to my age and leave you three to work it out with your dates." He replied to Jacob.

"It is fine." Charles said. "Thank you, Paul. Let me know if you find the assignment too confining."

"Remember, not a word of this to Olivia. I don't want to embarrass her. Oh, by the way, do you mind if she dances with other men?" Paul asked.

"If she wants to, let her." Charles said. "Just make sure none of them wander off with her outside."

"And if she wants fresh air at any point, should I bring her back to one of you?" He asked.

"No, you take her." Charles said.

"Well, enjoy the evening." Paul left them and came to me. "Miss Olivia, may I be your escort tonight?"

"My brothers will be watching." I told him.

"Your brothers arranged this." He smiled.

"They did? Was it you who stopped them from attacking me when I arrived?" I asked.

"Of course. I was watching for you from the balcony. When I noticed no one came with you, I wanted to find out why. I walked in on their argument and took advantage of the situation. I would have come to get you, but I see your independent thinking got us both what we wanted." He offered his hand to me and I took it. "You are truly the most beautiful woman at this celebration."

"Thank you for watching for me and for the compliment. I had the butler arrange my transportation." I told him.

"None of them will ever admit that to your father." Paul said.

"I know. I told the butler Charles was waiting for me." I smiled. "Then I sent the carriage home. I suppose someone will have to escort me home now."

"I would be delighted." Paul offered. "Shall we dance?"

Paul danced the first two dances with me. Then Charles wanted to dance with me to scold me. I expected it.

"What you did to get here was unwise, Olivia." Charles said as we danced.

"Charles, Keith and Jacob were fighting so fiercely I didn't want them to start hitting each other. I was an inconvenience as always and I had no intention of missing this celebration. I have looked forward to it for a month. I made my own dress. There was no harm done. I'm here having a good time and I am safe. Paul has been a good friend to me. He is very kind. I know he is doing you all a favor by watching over me. Father need never know about this. Now please let me have a good time dancing while you enjoy your evening with Sarah. I've agreed to let Paul dance with others when he chooses to do so. Nothing will happen to me. Do as Father asked. Give me some freedom." I insisted.

"Very well. Is the carriage waiting for you?" He asked me.

"No, I sent it back home. Was it supposed to wait for me?" I asked him.

He was frustrated. "We will work it out later. Don't disappear with anyone. If you want to leave before us make sure you come to see me first."

"I promise." I told him. "Charles, Aunt Lucille just arrived with Uncle Peter. I'll go say hello to them after this dance."

"Enjoy yourself." Charles told me as the dance ended.

I walked to meet my aunt and uncle.

"You look beautiful, Olivia. Where are your brothers? Shouldn't one of them be by your side?" My aunt asked.

"No, not tonight. We have new rules in place. I'm allowed some freedom and they have dates." I said cheerfully.

"My, my. That is news." Uncle Peter remarked.

A young man approached me. "Excuse me, Miss Olivia. My name is Alfred Pontie. May I have the next dance?"

I smiled at him. "Yes, you may." I took his hand.

"Have a nice time, Olivia." My aunt said as we went out to the dance floor.

The music was lively and I was dancing and jumping with the best of them. It was great fun. Paul kept a watchful eye. We had agreed not to give the impression that we were serious about each other. I danced a few more dances with younger men while he danced a few dances with older women. My brothers looked on occasionally and didn't worry. They always saw Paul nearby.

He finally came back to me. "Have you had your fill of the attention of these other young men?"

"Not necessarily." I answered.

"What? Should I be jealous now?" He held me closer as we waited for the next dance.

"Maybe. Some of them have been very nice to me. I admit I like the attention. I've never had attention before."

"Come now, Olivia. Are you teasing me or serious?" He asked.

"I'm not sure. Are you very upset with me?" I asked him.

"No, not really. You've never had attention. I thought this might happen." He said.

"And how are you going to handle it?" I asked him.

"I will be your brother's friend and strive to gain the trust of your family. When you wake up and realize I am the only man in your life who truly adores you, I'll be in a position to do something about it. In the meantime, you enjoy your new found freedom. Just be careful. Some of these men want to take advantage of you. If that happens, you take this as good advice; get rid of them. No second chances." He advised.

"Thank you, Paul." As I kissed him on the cheek Keith saw it.

"Big mistake, my dear. You have set off the warning bell for your brother Keith." He told me.

"Should we run?" I asked him.

"No, just tell him the truth. I was giving you advice and you appreciated it." Paul told me.

Keith pulled me away from him. His grip on my arm hurt me.

"Keith, don't embarrass her." Paul tried to calm him down. "It was an innocent kiss on the cheek. You are overreacting."

Keith turned around furious with him. "Back away."

Paul backed away.

"What are you doing kissing him? Is something going on?" He asked.

"No. He's been a perfect gentleman all evening and a good friend. My gosh Keith, he is as old as Charles. He gave me good advice about the young men here and I appreciated it. That's all. It was an innocent kiss. There was nothing romantic about it. You have misjudged me and certainly misjudged him. How could you pull me away like that? I'm not a possession. I'm your sister. I've done nothing wrong. You owe me an apology and you owe Paul one too." I was humiliated.

"I'm sorry, Olivia. You're right. I overreacted. I will apologize to Paul too." Keith escorted me back to Paul. "I apologize, Paul. I misjudged the situation."

"Yes you did." Paul was upset with him as he left to return to his date. "Are you alright, Olivia?"

"I'd like to go home. I've been humiliated enough tonight." I looked around at the staring eyes. "I have to tell Charles."

"I would be happy to escort you home if you need an escort." Paul offered.

"Let me talk to Charles about it first." I told him as I left his side.

Paul found Keith. "Brother or not, if you handle her like that again, I will put you down." Paul warned him and then followed after me.

Keith understood how angry Paul was so he walked away. He regretted that he had ruined my evening and made a horrible impression on his date Danielle.

"Charles, I want to leave." I told him.

He could see how upset I was. "What happened?"

"Keith humiliated me in front of a whole room of people. He dragged me away from Paul by my arm like a beast. I want to go home." He saw the tears filling my eyes.

Paul came to my side. "It was a misunderstanding Charles. I offered Olivia advice about the younger men here and she appreciated it. I just wanted her to be aware that not all of them are nice in the end. She thanked me and innocently kissed me on the cheek. Keith overreacted. When he understood the explanation, he apologized; but the damage was already done. He humiliated and embarrassed her." Paul explained.

"Charles, I cannot stay." I told him.

"Alright, I'll take you home." Charles offered.

"Charles, will you be leaving me here alone?" Sarah asked.

"Charles, if you won't mind, I can take Olivia home. It's not that far. I promise she will be safe. I have to come right back anyway. I'll let you know when I return." Paul offered.

"Thank you, Paul. Olivia, I'm sorry. I'll talk to Keith about his behavior tonight." Charles offered. "Goodnight, sweetheart."

"Please, Paul, let's leave now." I wanted to get away.

He took me out to his carriage and opened the door. He told the driver where to take us and he climbed in beside me. "I'm sorry, Olivia. What a life you've had being sheltered under that kind of domination. I feel very sad for you."

"Me too." I agreed.

"Is there anything I can do to help you?" He asked.

"No. This is just my life. I have to accept it." I told him.

"Imagine getting into trouble for something that wasn't even a romantic kiss. It's absurd." He was frustrated with the situation.

"You know what? You're right. If my brother wants to drag me around and embarrass me for no reason, let my heart discover the reason. Paul, please kiss me. I'm tired of being ruled over and abused. I might as well do something that deserved that kind of treatment." I said boldly.

"Olivia, you don't mean that." He said.

"Yes, I do. I do mean it. You said you wanted to help me. This will help me. I'm sure of it." I told him.

"Now you are acting like a child. Don't let a man take advantage of you to prove a point to the invisible. Your first kiss should be the best kiss you've ever had for all the right reasons." He lectured me.

I started crying. "Just one more man in my life to overshadow me with advice about how young and naïve I am. I will add your name to the list."

"Olivia, please don't be upset with me. You are breaking my heart. I just don't want you to regret this." He said sweetly.

"You are just like Charles and you don't even realize it." I wiped my tears.

He put his hand under my chin and lifted it so that he could kiss me. I felt his lips against mine. He was gentle and exciting to me as he kissed me once and again.

He looked at me when he stopped and whispered. "Revenge never tastes sweet, Olivia. I regret you have made me part of your plan and taken a kiss meant for love and given it a meaning it did not deserve or desire."

I stared at him. I was saddened by the truth of his words.

"Olivia, you are a torture to my soul. Please promise me that you won't seek revenge again this way. The idea that you would want to give yourself to a man to get even with your brother will worry me to death." Paul said.

"I won't. I promise. I'm very sorry. You were right to refuse me. I forced you by my words. Now I regret all of it."

He sat back against the seat in silence.

"I know that I have been a child about this tonight. To ask this would seem worse somehow, but I don't want this night to end with a kiss of revenge on my lips or yours. Please forgive me for imposing on you. Paul, could you help my heart and kiss me again because you care for me and not because of Keith?"

He leaned toward me and kissed me again and then again. It was more wonderful this time.

"I hope I haven't imposed on you too much." I told him.

"This was the perfect ending to this evening. I really do care about you, Olivia. I will be thinking about the touch of your lips for days, even weeks maybe. We are almost at your home. Forgive Keith. He will need your forgiveness. Please do not tell your brothers that we shared a kiss. I want to live to my next birthday." Paul smiled.

I laughed. "I shall never tell anyone of this. You have healed my heart and taught me well. I am a child in more ways than I realized. You deserve a grown up in your life. I will strive to be one next time."

He kissed the back of my hand. "Don't rush the process so much that we lose who you really are. Take your time Olivia. I want you to enjoy the journey. I'll be waiting at the end of it."

When we pulled up in front of my house, he helped me out of the carriage and walked me to the door. He waited until I was safely inside; then he left to return to the party. He went directly to Charles upon his return and told him that I got home safely.

"How was she?" Charles asked.

"Sad and upset about Keith." Paul answered. "I spoke to her about forgiving him. Charles, brother or not, if Keith handles her like that again in my presence, I won't back away. No one should treat any woman like that. You really need to discuss that with him."

"I will. Thank you for going out of your way for us tonight. I appreciate it." Charles went back to his date.

I dressed for bed and sat by my window looking out at the stars. I had no choice in my heart but to think about Paul and what he said. I looked at my hand and wondered if it had appeared to him to be the hand of a child or a woman when he kissed it. I was in the window longer than I realized. I heard my father's carriage approaching the house. I knew he would ask me questions if he was aware that I was awake. I blew out my lantern and climbed into bed quickly.

Chapter Four

The next morning, I rose from my bed early and asked the servants to draw me a bath in my room. I was soaking in the tub as the sun rose in the sky. I knew breakfast for my brothers would be soon. I could hear father already walking the hall and proceeding downstairs to wait for them.

I stood up in the tub and grabbed a wrap for my body and stepped out of the tub. Just then my door opened.

"Keith, leave me. I'm not dressed." I said it softly as I knew he would be in great trouble if my father heard my words. I was surprised when he entered my room and shut the door. "What are you doing?"

"Olivia, I came to apologize for last night. Did I do that to your arm?" He saw the bruise on my left arm and touched it.

"Have you gone mad? I'm not dressed. Get out!" I insisted as I turned my back to him.

"Yes, of course." He backed away from me. "Olivia, I'm truly sorry."

"Get out!" I insisted in a whispered tone.

He shut the door as he left. I was still unsettled about his actions. It was like he was a different unexpected kind of person. I was concerned that I couldn't trust him.

Jacob saw him coming out of my room. "What were you doing in there?" He asked him. "Did you wake Olivia?"

"She was already awake." Keith said as he rushed toward the staircase.

Jacob let him get away from him. He knocked on my door. "Olivia, may I come in?"

I wasn't aware that he had seen Keith coming out of my room. "No, Jacob, I've just taken a bath and I'm not dressed."

"Olivia, come to the door please. I must speak with you." He said.

"Can it wait?" I asked him.

"No, it cannot. Please Olivia, come to the door." Jacob insisted.

I cracked the door. "What is it?"

"I saw Keith coming out of your room. Were you in the tub when he was in there?" Jacob asked.

"No, Jacob. I don't understand him this morning. He came into my room without knocking. When he saw that I was wearing only a wrap, he entered and shut the door to talk to me. Even when I insisted that he leave, he hesitated. He wanted to apologize for last night. I had to insist more than once. What is wrong with him? He is surely not himself." I explained.

"Olivia, what happened last night?" Jacob asked.

"Oh, Jacob, can I refuse to tell you?" I asked.

"Not this morning. Not after Keith's behavior. I need to know." He insisted.

"I gave Paul an innocent kiss on the cheek to thank him for being so nice as to offer me advice about young men. He told me to beware of those who would want to take advantage of me, and I appreciated it. Keith saw it happen, and he grabbed me so harshly it bruised my arm. He embarrassed me in front of a room full of people as he demanded an explanation. I left early." I told him.

I saw the anger growing in my brother.

"Please Jacob, don't tell Father." I begged him. "He will be so upset with me. You know he is waiting for a reason to put me under lock and key again, and I've done nothing wrong. If you must say anything to anyone, tell Charles or have it out with Keith alone. I beg of you."

Jacob calmed down. "I will let this go for now. I will keep it to myself until I have the matter settled in my heart. If you wish to spare Keith, cover your arm with clothing."

"Thank you, Jacob." I was relieved.

"Olivia, I regret to say this but you must not trust Keith after today. Lock your door at night and keep it locked until you are dressed and coming out of it. I don't know what is happening with him. Take this morning as a type of warning to you." Jacob told me. "If anyone should inquire about it, just tell them that it is something you decided on and you are comfortable with it."

"I will. Thank you, Jacob. I will be down in a few minutes." I told him.

I watched him leave the door and proceed down the staircase. I closed my door and locked it. Then I dressed to join them for breakfast.

"Did you have a good time at the celebration last night, Olivia?" My father asked as I joined them for breakfast.

"Yes, Father. It was quite a joyous occasion. Mr. and Mrs. Stephens were very happy with the turnout." I told him.

"Glad to hear it." He went on with his breakfast. "I'll be away for a few weeks. When I return I will have good news to share with all of you."

"Sounds like a mystery, Father. Are you sure you cannot give us a hint?" I asked him.

"No, no hint." He smiled.

"When will you be leaving?" I asked him.

"Tonight." He answered. "Keith is in charge while I am away. If there is a matter that you cannot handle, take the matter up with Charles."

"Yes Sir." Keith replied.

My father looked around the room. "I may be gone quite often, but I know when there is an undercurrent of something between my children. What is going on?" He asked.

"Keith and I have an important matter to discuss, a disagreement of sorts. We choose to handle it ourselves." Jacob told him.

"And why are you so distressed, Olivia?" He asked me.

"Father, I hate it when they argue. I'm afraid they might hurt each other." I told him.

"Handle it like gentlemen. I don't want to come back to broken noses and black eyes." My father warned them.

"I'm sure we can work it out, Father." Keith said.

My father took my hand gently in his. "Not to worry, Olivia, in the end they are still brothers."

I smiled at him. "Yes, Father. I shall be sure to remind them of it."

He wiped his mouth with his napkin. Then he got up and kissed me on the cheek. "I shall be thinking of all of you while I am away. I have meetings to attend. Keith, Jacob, follow me out to the carriage. I have instructions for both of you."

Each of my brothers got up to follow him outside. As soon as he left, Jacob demanded that Keith walk with him.

"I will talk to you privately or out in the open, but we will talk." Jacob told him.

Keith followed him. "What is it?"

"How dare you enter our sister's room when she is not dressed. What is wrong with you? You know better." Jacob yelled at him.

47

"I had no devious plan when I went into her room. I went in there to apologize." Keith told him.

"For bruising her arm." Jacob accused him. "We don't handle our sister in that manner. What would cause you to treat her so violently and then intrude on her privacy?"

"Jacob, I admit I was wrong to handle her that way. I had too much wine. That and the shock I felt when I saw her kissing Paul caused me to lose my senses. We've been pressured to keep watch over her for years. She has been our responsibility; and the first evening she receives some sort of freedom, she kisses her dance partner on the cheek. It infuriated me that she had become a flirt so quickly." Keith explained.

"Are you not familiar with our sister? She is well-mannered and sweet. An explanation of her intention could have been handled without embarrassing her." Jacob lectured him.

"I know that now. I felt bad about my behavior. I wanted desperately to apologize to her. I know she is a beautiful woman, but we are her brothers. I don't see her through romantic eyes. She is still my little sister. I do need to apologize for invading her privacy. I seem to be making a series of mistakes toward Olivia. I promise you and I will promise her that my behavior will never be as intrusive as it has been these last two days." Keith told him.

"I've advised Olivia to lock her bedroom door from now on. I am not convinced that this will not happen again." Jacob told him.

"Jacob, I am her brother. I would not go after my own sister." Keith was insulted and offended.

"That's just it, Keith; you are not her brother and you know that. Father knows it. Charles knows it, and I know it. The only one who is not aware of how you entered this family is Olivia." Jacob reminded him.

"So with two mistakes to my credit, you have disowned me as your brother and cast me out of your good grace?" Keith was angry.

"I am merely stating a fact. We have always considered you our brother. I still consider you my brother. What I am no longer sure of is if you consider yourself Olivia's brother. If you are bordering on seeing her differently, then it is my duty to both of you to prevent a tragedy in this house. Her bedroom door will remain locked when she is in her bedroom. If you overstep again, I will take the matter up with Father. The only reason I did not do that this morning is because Olivia would have suffered from that disclosure." Jacob warned him.

"Consider me warned." Keith walked away. He found me in the sitting room reading. He sat down beside me. "Olivia, I seem to be apologizing to you continually. I realize I haven't been myself these last few days. I was drinking at the party and I lost control of my senses. I should have asked for your company politely and had you explain the kiss. I'm very sorry I hurt you. You know I love you. I will be more careful of you in the future. About this morning, I had no right to walk into your room without your invitation. I see you as my little sister. We played together growing up, and I have been purposefully trying to protect you all your life. It didn't occur to me this morning that you were any older than that little girl. I was so focused on apologizing that I disregarded what I actually saw. I am very sorry for my treatment of you. You have become a beautiful young woman. I am very proud to be your brother. I will knock next time and wait for an invitation to enter your room. I'm very sorry. Please forgive me." Keith said sincerely.

I smiled at him and kissed him on the cheek. "You are forgiven."

"Thank you." He stood up. "I have to go off to work. Enjoy your day."

"Have a good day, Keith." I watched him walk out of the room.

Jacob came to see me immediately after he left. "Olivia, I have spoken with Keith. He explained about drinking last night. He also tried to convince me that he only saw you as a little girl. That may be true, but I have my doubts. No one knows the heart of a man except himself and God. I cannot understand how Keith could picture you as anything other than how you actually appear. I cannot wrap my thoughts around that explanation. I just wanted you to know that I have decided not to tell Father or Charles about this. I think my words to Keith had an effect. Olivia, I swear I will protect you. If anything like what happened this morning happens again with Keith, promise me that you will come to me immediately." Jacob said.

"I promise." I told him.

"Don't ever let shame or embarrassment keep you from telling me." Jacob told her.

"I really believe his apology was sincere. I will keep my bedroom door locked; and I promise that no matter how I feel,

I will tell you should it happen again. Jacob, please don't worry. I can tell that you are still upset by this. Give Keith the benefit of the doubt. His apology was sincere."

He kissed me on the cheek. "How could I ever deny you? Alright, I will let it go. I will see you later this evening. Be good." It seemed to be an amusing warning.

I laughed. "I will. Thank you, Jacob. I love you."

He smiled and left.

A few hours went by quietly. Then the butler announced that Sarah and a few of her friends were at the door and wanted to visit with me.

"Send them in please." I told the butler.

They entered the room. Sarah came to me first. "Olivia, I'm so glad you agreed to see us."

"This is a delightful surprise." I told her.

"Olivia, this is Janet Zachery and my friend Prudence Tiller." She introduced them.

"Ladies, please sit." I invited them.

"Actually, Olivia, we came to invite you to join us. We loved the dress you wore last night and Charles told me that you designed it yourself and put it together. The girls and I agree that there was no more beautiful a creation than that dress at the celebration. You have a creative eye and such talent. We would like you to help us pick out material for fancy dresses for each of us. We were wondering if you might consider giving us lessons as to how to design our own dresses and put them together. Would you be interested in that? If you want to be paid for the lessons, we would be willing to pay you. We hate to impose, but the dress was so beautiful and you looked beautiful in it." Sarah said and the girls agreed.

"This is such a surprise." I told them.

"We are prepared to beg." Prudence offered.

I laughed. "No need. I would be delighted to help you. This won't be easy work. I will help you and guide you, but I won't stitch your dress. The work must be done by you alone."

Sarah offered her hand and smiled. "It's a deal." She said as I shook her hand.

"We should smoke a cigar now." Janet suggested and we laughed.

"Can you come now? I have a carriage waiting for us." Sarah told me.

"Let me leave a note for my brother, and I will join you." I told her. I was excited to have potential friends and to go out on the town with them alone and unprotected. I knew Father would be busy all day. I wrote a note to Keith and left it with the butler.

"Miss Olivia, are you sure this is wise?" The butler whispered.

"Probably not, but I am going anyway." I smiled and left with the girls.

We chatted all the way into town. The driver let us off at the edge of the market place. We looked through volumes of material and lace.

"Olivia, how will we know how much to buy?" Janet asked.

"I have the designs in my head. I know how much you will need." I assured her.

"You must be a creative genius." Prudence remarked.

"No, just a girl who has had too much time to herself growing up." I replied. I turned around and Paul was right in front of me. "Oh!"

"Good afternoon, Miss Olivia." He smiled.

"What are you doing here?" I asked him.

"I was on my way from a meeting with your father. I'm sure he would be interested to find out you were out on the town with these beautiful ladies." He said cheerfully.

"Freedom has its rewards." I told him.

"Yes, I'm sure it does." He agreed.

"Mr. Stephens, your parents' celebration was wonderful." Sarah told him.

"Please call me Paul, Miss Sarah." He insisted.

"Paul, we've kidnapped Olivia. We had admired her dress last night and asked her if she would help us design one for ourselves in advance of the next social gathering." Janet explained.

"It is true. She looked stunning in that dress. I believe it was more her natural beauty that made the dress look radiant than the other way around." He was charming, and the other girls adored his manner.

"Do you intend to follow us around, Mr. Stephens?" I asked him as he walked with me.

"I intend to follow you around, Miss Douglas." He whispered. "Remember, I am trying to earn the good grace of your very own father."

I laughed. "Very well, but you may become bored as we ignore your presence."

"You just carry on. I will not be far away." He backed away from us.

"What is it about you that makes men want to protect you?" Sarah asked me.

"Knowing my father would explain most of it." I told them. "Come this way. There are more selections of material in this section."

The girls followed me as Paul followed the girls.

When Keith returned home the butler handed him my note. He was not happy. He left immediately to go to the market place. Paul was watching me smile and laugh when he saw Keith get off his horse in a determined manner to find me. He intercepted him.

"Keith, don't make the same mistake you made last night. Olivia is having a joyous time with the ladies. I've been keeping an eye on her from a distance since she arrived in the market place. Don't embarrass her."

"How is it you happen to be her guardian today?" He asked.

"Just coincidence. I was traveling through the market place after I left a meeting with your father this morning. I had no pressing engagements and I am aware of your father's insistence to protect Olivia. I shall leave if you wish to take my place. I must say the study of young giggling women is quite delightful. They are amazed at the strangest things in life. It's quite an education and, besides, Prudence is adorable. I may ask her to dine with me." Paul told him.

"Are you sure you don't mind? I have an important appointment I did not want to have to cancel." Keith said.

"No problem. My afternoon is clear of meetings and appointments. I am enjoying the entertainment as ridiculous as it is." Paul said.

"Thank you, Paul. I appreciate this." Keith said.

"Not a problem. Go on now. Don't be late for your appointment." Paul said.

After we had finished shopping Paul escorted me to the carriage. "I trust you will all be returning home now that you have the raw materials for your amazing new creations." He said.

"Yes." Prudence answered. "We appreciate your guardianship."

"My pleasure. You were unaware, but I did turn away a cruel looking man who had his eye on you." He told us.

"I don't believe you." I laughed.

"Dear Lady, a protector of such beauty would never lie." He said as he closed the carriage door.

As the carriage pulled away, Prudence asked, "Do you believe him?"

"It could have happened." Janet said.

"I am telling you, he is lying." I insisted.

The girls promised me they would come back to my home the next day in the late morning to get started on their dresses. I was thrilled to have female company and especially their friendship.

Keith walked into the house shortly after I did. "Olivia, I'm sure Father did not mean that you could go off to the market place without an escort."

"Keith, I was in the company of three other women. I wasn't alone and Paul Stephens showed up almost immediately after we arrived. He was quite the gentleman to watch over us from a distance. I'm sure Father would have approved of that." I told him.

"I know. I was just about to address your freedom when he stepped in and stopped me from making another mistake. I'm glad he was there, but really, Olivia, you need an escort." Keith insisted.

"What am I to do? Wait around for you or Jacob to come home in the middle of the day? You know that will keep me locked up in the house forever. Keith, I'm going out with the girls if they invite me. I will leave you a note, but I am going." I insisted.

"Then I will have no choice but to lock you in your room during the day." He said.

"You wouldn't dare." I objected.

"Yes Olivia, I would. You have no idea of the dangers in town. There are thieves and all types of criminals in the streets. You girls are being naïve." He insisted.

"You're impossible. The first sign that I can enjoy my life and you are taking it away from me. I will not be a prisoner in my own home." I ran from the room crying. I went up to my bedroom and locked the door.

"Great, another drama in the house." Keith worried.

Father left for his trip before supper. Jacob and Keith ate alone. I refused to come down and join them.

"Is she ill?" Jacob asked the servant.

"No Sir." The servant replied.

Keith dismissed the servant. "She's angry." He told Jacob.

"Why?" He asked.

"She went into town today with three other women. They were shopping in the market place without an escort. I went to pull her back to the house, but Paul Stephens interrupted that plan. He had just finished a meeting with father. He was on his way through the market place when he spotted her with her friends. He stayed in the shadows and watched over her for us. When she got home, I forbid her to go into town again without an escort. She refused to listen, so I threatened to lock her in her room. She is angry with us. She wants her freedom. Jacob, you know the people who hang around the market place. It's not safe for her there." Keith said.

"I know, but we cannot keep her a prisoner in this house. There has to be a way to protect her outside the house." He said as he picked up his glass to drink.

"Jacob before Father took me in, do you remember when he brought Olivia home as a baby?" Keith asked.

"Not really, I barely remember you being brought home. I was under three years old. I know the same story you do. He was on a trip with mother while she was pregnant, and mother died. He just brought Olivia back home with him. Why do you ask?"

"I met some men recently. They raised some questions about Olivia." Keith said.

"What kinds of questions?" Jacob asked.

"Please promise me you won't be angry. I need your wisdom with this, not your wrath." Keith told him.

"I promise. Explain what you know." Jacob listened.

"A few days ago, a group of well-dressed men from France arranged to meet with me. They confirmed some of what we know. Father was in France when your mother was due to give birth to Olivia. They explained that at that same time, a Duchess in that country gave birth to a baby girl. The story they tell is that this Duchess Dupree was married to a Duke who was in line to the throne of France. He was accused of conspiring against the King of France. The King ordered him to his death. His intention was to kill the Duchess also and her unborn child. The Duchess gave birth to a daughter the same night as your mother and sister died in childbirth. Father was beside himself with grief, and in that grief he stole Olivia from the Duchess and called her his own. They claim the Duchess has been looking for Olivia since then. She was delayed in her search as she had to find a way to clear her husband's name first. With the help of another person of importance, she was able to do that. His name escapes me now. These men are here for Olivia. They want to return her to the Duchess. I was made aware of this days before the celebration. I didn't believe them, but the story weighed heavy on my heart. The daughter of the Duchess has a birthmark near the back of her left shoulder blade toward the middle of her back. It was supposed to resemble the shape of a butterfly. I'm sorry I lied to you before. I didn't go after Olivia because I was angry about the kiss she gave Paul. I went after her so that I would have a reason to apologize to her the next day. I knew she was in the tub. I waited outside her door until I could hear her get out of the tub. I took the chance that she was wrapped when I entered her room. I approached her so that I could get a good look at her and verify the birthmark. Jacob, she has the birthmark. None of us knew that about her. She has been covered since birth. Only nursemaids and her governess have seen the birthmark. If their story is true, she belongs to someone else and not with us." Keith told him.

"Do you believe this story?" Jacob asked him.

"What reason would they have to lie? They are very well dressed. They seem important. They don't want to frighten her. They want her to go back with them willingly." He explained.

"Why didn't you tell this to Father?" Jacob asked him.

"I had to know for myself first if there was a possibility the story was true. How do I approach Father with this? Their whole claim is that he stole her from the Duchess. How do I tell him now how I happen to know about the birthmark?" Keith asked.

"The question I have is why did they approach you and not Charles or me? Why you?" Jacob asked.

"I don't know." Keith answered.

"While they are out there, we can't trust that they won't grab Olivia and just take her back with them." Jacob said. "Keith, you knew this before today. Why didn't you drag her back here? Paul Stephens would not be able to handle a group of men coming after Olivia."

"They promised me that they would not take her. They wanted to give me time to check out the story and find a way to get Olivia to agree to go back. Paul Stephens is much more clever than you think he is. I've done a little research on him. It is only a rumor that he has relatives in France. I haven't been able to verify the rumor. Mr. and Mrs. Stephens have a lavish home here, but they claim all their sons live in France. At the celebration none of them were present except Paul. You would think that on so special an anniversary their other sons would have shown up. Some things about that family just don't add up. Mr. Stephens has been a friend of our father for two years. He started out advising father about the security in our house. He came to us as an expert; but after a year here, he started a business that has nothing to do with protection or security. Maybe the Stephens family is connected to the Duchess somehow. I wouldn't be surprised if Paul Stephens isn't part of this plan to bring Olivia back to the Duchess. My belief is that no one will bother Olivia while Paul is nearby. They risk too much to injure a man connected to the Duchess." Keith said.

"You have to tell Father all this. Let him clear his own good name. Do you know how to get hold of him?" Jacob asked.

"Usually he leaves a schedule of where he will be stopping, but not this time. I have no idea where he went." Keith said.

"We must tell Charles and inform him about Paul Stephens." Jacob said.

"I've already sent for him." Keith said.

I entered the room. "Really, you believe I am the daughter of a Duchess Dupree?" I surprised them.

"Olivia, how long have you been listening?" Jacob asked me.

"I'm quite sure I've been listening since you started this conversation."

"It might be a horrid story, Olivia, with very little truth." Jacob said.

"Send for Paul Stephens. He will tell me the truth." I told them.

"Olivia, we should discuss this with Charles and Father first." Jacob said.

"No, Jacob. This is about me. Send for Paul Stephens or I will." I insisted.

"Wait until Charles gets here Olivia. Then we will send for Paul." Keith said.

"Very well. Let me know when he gets here. I want to talk to him." I left the room and then the house unnoticed. I saddled my own horse from the stable and rode to Paul's home. Mr. and Mrs. Stephens were surprised that I was at their door alone.

"Olivia, come in. It's late dear. What are you doing here alone?" Mrs. Stephens asked.

"I came to see Paul about an urgent matter. Is he here?" I asked them.

"He came back from a ride. He is in the stables taking care of his horse. We can send for him." Mrs. Stephens offered.

"May I just go to him? It is very important." I asked them.

"Of course." Mrs. Stephens said. She walked me to the back door and handed me a lantern. "Be very careful where you step."

"Thank you." I left the house and walked to the stables. I found Paul brushing down his horse. "Paul."

He turned around surprised. "Are you here with your brothers?"

"No, just me." I answered.

"How did you get here?" He asked.

"My horse." I answered.

"Are you insane? You shouldn't be out on a horse after dark alone. It's dangerous." He stopped brushing the horse and came closer to me.

"I need to speak to you. It's very important." I told him.

He dismissed the staff in the barn. "Leave us." He ordered them. Then he invited me to sit with him on a clean stack of hay. "What is so important that you would risk your safety to see me?"

I explained the story that I had overheard. "Are you involved in this? Do you know if it is true?"

"Some of it is, and some of it is not." He said.

"Tell me. I will believe you."

"Olivia, I believe you are your father's daughter. You do not belong to the Duchess Dupree. On the night you were born it is true that your mother and the Duchess gave birth to girls. According to your father's story, which I've only heard from another, her child did not live very long and those attending the child noticed that the baby girl did have a birthmark that resembled a butterfly on her back near her shoulder blade. The Duke was already dead, and the Duchess escaped execution after the birth of her child by fleeing with a nurse and her dying baby girl in her arms. Your mother held on to deliver you into this world before she died. Your father hired a wet nurse immediately. He mourned her as he saw to it that she had a proper burial. Then he brought you home. Years later, the Duke was cleared of all wrong doing. The Duchess was restored, but her husband's property could only be restored to his heir. She had no child from him, so she made up this story to keep those in charge of the estate from taking it away from her. The Duke's estate has guardians over it. The powers that be informed the Duchess that she had until the eighteenth birthday of her daughter to find her and bring her back to claim the estate. You were close to a year old when you were taken from your home. The mark you have on your back is not a birthmark, but a mark made by your kidnappers to resemble the butterfly birthmark of the true heir. It was the result of the efforts of the people who kidnapped you. Your father got you back purely from the rescue efforts of a young orphan boy named Keith. He was so grateful to the boy that he raised him as your brother. Keith has been looking after you for years. After the kidnapping, your father moved your family around constantly. Then a few years ago he settled here."

"This is amazing. How do you know all this?" I asked him.

"My father is a very informative man. He was hired by your father a few years ago to make your home more secure. Your father knows of the efforts to bring you to the Duchess before your eighteenth birthday. My father was in charge of hiring those who watched over you. My father learned what he could from your father. He was curious about the specifics, so he wrote to me and asked me to check out the story. I've told no one but you. While I was studying the wine business I heard the other side of the story. In France the people are convinced that the daughter of the Duchess is still alive. I put what I already knew together with what I learned while I was there. I admit that I still have questions, but I realized that an extraordinary young woman was in danger. I had to find out for myself. The wine I am representing helped me to gain a connection to your family. Once I met them and you, I was more convinced that your Father was telling the truth. At first glance you had my heart. I know how to defend myself with weapons and I'm very good defending myself with my hands. I have connections to the best and the worst of people around here. I'm never really alone." He snapped his fingers and two men came out into the open to reveal their presence to me. Then he waved them away. "You can be sure that an attempt to take you back to the Duchess will happen before your eighteenth birthday. I intend to prevent that attempt from being successful." He said.

"Paul, now that I know the truth, how can the Duchess pass me off as her daughter? I would just reveal to them who I really am, and my father would not give up until he got me back."

"You underestimate how desperate Duchess Dupree is to get her estate back." Paul said. "She can prove by the mark on your back and the date of your birthday that you are her child. They will believe her and not you." Paul told me.

"Other than protecting me and trying to prevent her from kidnapping me, is there any other way to spoil her plans?" I asked him.

"Yes, but you won't like it." He said.

"What is it?" I asked him.

"You get married before she takes you. Then your husband would inherit her estate. If he died, only your heir could get the estate. Since you are not with child, your life and his would be protected." He explained.

"Good." I said.

"What do you mean good?" He asked.

"I do have a plan." I said.

"What kind of plan?" He asked.

"I will pretend to marry my brother Keith. I trust him. He has been with me all of my life. You said it yourself that he really isn't my brother. Father could arrange it." I told him.

"No, you are not doing that." He insisted.

"Why not?" I asked.

"For one, his name is Douglas. There is too much paper work that would need to be rectified and rearranged. He risks losing any inheritance your father would leave him. His reputation as the son of Sir Douglas would be ruined. Last of all, he is a man. Once the bonds of brotherhood are broken he is just a man lying next to a woman. You get that idea right out of your head." Paul was very upset.

One of Paul's companions brought a note to him. He read it and was more upset.

"What's wrong?" I asked him.

"That surprise your father told you about - the one he was bringing home in two weeks, I just found out what it is." He said.

"Why did you even want to know?" I asked him.

"Olivia, I care about protecting you. Your father has been

aware of the plans of the Duchess. He knows the best way to protect you is to make sure you are married. He found you a husband. He has arranged a marriage for you with the son of Earl Thomas Yates. You are destined to become the future bride of Marvin Yates." He told me.

"What an awful name." I said.

"You'll have the heritage and be stuck in a loveless marriage to a complete stranger. For sure he will move you to France and with his title and you in his bed, he will easily elevate himself." He explained.

"I am so tired of people making life decisions for me. All my life I have been sheltered and ruled. Now, when I think I have some freedom to enjoy my life, this happens. My Father thinks of one more way to rule my life and give me more agony." I complained. "I will just refuse to marry him." I declared.

"Then you had better prepare yourself for a fight with your father and your brothers." He warned me.

We were interrupted by Paul's father. "Paul, Charles Douglas is here to see you. He is at the house. He spotted Olivia's horse. He is not in a pleasant mood." His father warned as he came into the stable.

"Come, Olivia. It is time to pay for your independent thinking and your private meeting with me." Paul took my hand and walked with me to meet Charles in the house.

Mr. Stephens escorted us into the house and into the library where Charles was waiting. I could tell by his demeanor he was very angry.

"Father, we will be fine. Please shut the doors." Paul said.

His father shut the doors.

"I should like to take you over my knee, Olivia." Charles got in my face. "How could you run off like that alone? Keith and Jacob are frantic. They are searching the grounds and the town for you. I had to send word back to them that I found you."

"I'm sorry I worried you, but I needed to speak with Paul alone. I knew you three would gang up on him and it would just be a screaming match. I wanted the truth, not some version of it given in anger and accusations." I told him.

"Leave us." Charles ordered me.

"No, Charles, I will not leave you. Paul told me the truth. He told me all of it. He knows more of this story than any of us did. This meeting with me is not his fault. He came to protect me. Please sit down calmly. Let him explain the entire story of my birth and the Duchess to you. Let him tell you who he really is and what his true intentions are. There is no reason to fight or argue, and there is no reason for me to leave." I said.

"I want you out of this room, Olivia!" He yelled at me.

"And I said I refuse!" I screamed back at him.

He stepped toward me, and Paul got between us. "I let one brother bruise her up; I won't let another. I know you are angry. I understand you are upset, and Olivia is challenging your authority. Your pride is hurt. I get it. She is being stubborn and yelling at you because she is frightened to her core. A lot of things have changed in her life very quickly. We both know women can get emotional and fierce when they are fighting to survive. Let's give her what she wants this one time. Please, Charles." Paul persuaded him.

Charles sat down. "Tell me what you know."

Paul explained to him exactly what he had explained to me.

"So you believe that the only way to protect Olivia is to have her get married?" Charles asked.

"Charles, you can't let our Father marry me off to a stranger. Please don't let that happen. I will be miserable for the rest of my life." I pleaded with him.

"You love my sister, don't you?" He asked Paul.

"From the first moment I saw her." He answered.

"I knew it. You are too slick." Charles said.

"If I had told you the truth, you would have kept her completely out of my reach. You forced me to be clever. I told her that I was willing to wait for her to experience a little more life. I would have waited for her to come back to me." Paul said.

"We will watch over Olivia and protect her together. I need your help to do that." He told Paul. Then he spoke to me. "We will wait until Father gets home with Mr. Yates. You owe Father at least the time to get to know Mr. Yates. He may surprise you and be just the type of husband you want." Charles said.

"Charles, promise me that if I object to the match, you will fight for me and not against me." I begged him.

"Olivia, I can't make that promise." He said.

I turned to Paul. "Do you love me? Truly love me?"

"With all my heart." He said.

"Ask my brother to leave the room. I want to talk to you alone before I leave." I told him.

"Charles?" He didn't want to finish the request.

"I'll give you a few minutes." Charles left the room and closed the doors as he left.

"If I cannot get out of marrying Mr. Yates, will you rescue me?" I asked him.

"I can only rescue you, if you will marry me when I do." He said. "Otherwise, your Father will pull you right out of my hands."

"At the front of our house there is a statue of an angel. You know it, don't you?" I asked him.

"Yes." He answered.

"I will put jewelry on its arm if I need to be rescued. If you spot it, wait for me that evening. I will meet you at the fountain near the flower garden. Take me that night and marry me. I will be yours forever." I told him.

"I will be there." He promised.

"If you are in the house and available to me, the sign will be somewhat different. I have a little statue of an angel that I keep in my room. I will bring it down and put jewelry on it in front of you. Meet me that night. I won't stay in my house another night. If you don't come for me, I will run away to the harbor and get on a ship. I won't stay here to marry a man who will drag me off to the Duchess." I told him.

"I'll be watching the fountain just after the sun goes down. I'm praying you put the jewelry on that angel." He told me.

"I don't know how soon I will be able to sneak away, but I will come out. Please, Paul, seal our agreement with a kiss." I looked up at him.

He leaned down and kissed me like it was our last kiss. I didn't want to leave him.

"I love you." He whispered.

"I know you do. I am sorry to put you through any of this, but Charles is right. I do owe it to my father to consider the man he has chosen for me." I told him.

"I'm not happy about that decision, but I understand it." Then he walked me to the doors and opened them. Charles was waiting by the front door. "Goodnight Charles. I will be at your house just after sunrise. We can talk over how you want me to help you protect Olivia. We have two weeks to plan this."

Charles shook his hand and we left.

Chapter Five

For the next two weeks I worked quickly to help the girls cut and design their dresses. I left them each a pattern of how to sew them. They wondered why we were in such a hurry. I told them I expected my father to take me away on a vacation, and I wasn't sure when I would be back.

I visited with my Aunt Lucille and confided in her about everything, even Paul. She was very understanding and promised to keep my secret and pray for me. I loved her so much. We both were aware of what was at stake.

My father was surprised when he arrived to see Paul wandering around our house with me. "Paul, what are you doing here with Olivia, and where are my sons?"

"Charles asked me to watch over Olivia while he is at work. I told him I would." Paul answered.

I came in from the other room and hugged my father. "I'm glad you are home."

"Olivia, I would like you to meet Mr. Marvin Yates. He is the son of Earl Thomas Yates." My father smiled.

"I'm pleased to meet you, Mr. Yates." I said.

He bowed at the waist as I watched Paul raise his eyebrows. I almost laughed.

"The pleasure is mine, Miss Olivia. Please call me Marvin." He said.

My father turned toward the butler. "Send for my sons. Send word that I would like all of them to come home immediately. Have the cook prepare a special lunch for us."

"Yes, Sir Douglas." The butler replied and went to carry out his assignment.

"Paul has agreed to stay for lunch today, Father. He's been so gracious to watch over me." I told my father cheerfully.

"Paul Stephens is a business partner of mine. His father Trevor Stephens has been a friend of mine for years." He explained to Marvin.

"Very nice to meet you, Mr. Stephens." Marvin extended his hand to shake Paul's.

Paul grabbed it securely and shook his hand. "Are you just visiting this area, Mr. Yates?"

"It will be an extended stay. Sir Douglas has invited me to become acquainted with his family." Marvin told him.

"They are all very nice. We get along quite well." Paul told him.

Charles showed up first and then Jacob and Keith. My father introduced them to Marvin. Then he invited the family to eat lunch together. My father was very cheery and bragged about Marvin's wealth and station in life.

"Well, I told you that I would have a surprise for all of you. It is time I announced it." He said.

I braced myself and looked at Paul. He winked at me so that my father and Marvin would not notice.

"I have arranged with Earl Thomas Yates to grant a marriage between his son Marvin and our beloved Olivia." He announced it, and I fainted right off the chair just like Paul had told me to.

"Olivia!" My father was horrified as he rose with the rest of the men in the room to come to my aid.

"I'd say this was a bit of a shock to her." Keith said as he picked me up and carried me up to my bedroom.

"Do you think she will be alright?" Marvin asked Charles.

"I've never seen Olivia faint. I hope so." He sounded worried.

My father shouted orders at the servants to attend to me. "I'm sure she will be fine. It could be that we waited too long to eat and that the surprise was too much." He told Marvin.

"Sir Douglas, I was under the impression that Olivia wanted to get married." Marvin said.

"She does. She just didn't expect that I would find a suitable husband for her this quickly." He tried to cover for himself.

Paul smiled. Now he had a plan to sabotage the outcome of this romance. He slipped away and went to check on me. He knocked on my bedroom door, and Keith came to meet him.

"What?" Keith whispered.

"Let her know that Marvin was under the impression she wanted to get married." Paul whispered.

"I will. Tell my father she is coming around. It will give me a few minutes to tell her." Keith turned and went back into the room.

Paul came back into the dining room. "Sir Douglas, Keith met me in the hall. He said to tell you Olivia is coming around."

My father got up immediately and came to me. He cleared the room and sat down beside me on the bed. "How are you?" He asked.

"Father, I've embarrassed myself." I acted as if I was worried as I sat up.

"Nonsense. It was probably lack of food and the surprise. He is a wonderful man, Olivia. You will be well-off and have a title and land. It is all that I had hoped for you." He said.

"Father, am I the daughter of a French Duchess?" I asked him.

"Why would you ask such a question?" He asked.

"Father, many things have happened while you were gone. You must talk to Charles and the others about it. They have been guarding me from men who think I am the daughter of someone called Duchess Dupree." I told him.

"Olivia, you are my daughter. I was there at your birth by your mother's side. This Duchess is delusional. I will not let her have you or harm you in any way. I give you my word." He promised.

"Father, why would you bring a perfect stranger to our home and announce a wedding when I don't even know the man? I've barely gotten a taste of freedom, and now you want to put the chains of marriage on my wrists. I don't want to marry him. I don't even know him. I've never even been told about marriage or being a wife. I don't know anything about men or romance. Father, please send him away. I don't care about title and land. I want to experience freedom and affection first." I told him.

"That is the talk of a loose woman. You will not speak of such things again. I raised you better than that. You have an opportunity here to become someone special. I don't want a multitude of men to handle you. You were saved for one man and that man is Marvin." My father sounded cross.

"How could you say such things? I've never shamed you or myself. I know the difference between women who throw themselves at a man and women like me who are innocent of such things. I have no intention of bringing shame on myself or you. What you said, Father, is so unkind and I did not deserve it." I spoke boldly.

"What happened to my sweet Olivia? You would never talk to me in that tone of voice." He was surprised.

"You stopped loving me the moment you disregarded my needs for your own. I will not marry a stranger." I insisted.

He got up and slapped my face. "I am your Father! You will do what I tell you to do." He commanded as I cried. "You will clean your face and fix your hair. Then you will come downstairs and be very nice to Marvin. He will be your husband and you will welcome his attention. Get that settled in your heart. Do not speak to me that way again. I rule this house. After you marry Marvin, he will rule your home. This is settled. Now get up and stop that crying." He walked out of my room and slammed the door.

Everyone heard the door slam.

"They stick sometimes." Jacob said to Marvin.

Paul knew the argument had to have been bad. He was very concerned for me.

My father returned to the table calmly and smiled. "Olivia just needs a few moments. Please, everyone just enjoy your meal." He said cheerfully.

I came down to the table ten minutes later. I wore my hair down to cover the side of my face, but my brothers and Paul noticed the red. Fortunately, Marvin and my father did not.

"Marvin, are you a praying man?" I asked him.

"Yes, of course, Olivia. It is important for a man to seek God in all things." He said.

"I have had this little angel most of my life. I picture angels in heaven being adorned with jewels." I told him as I put a chain with a jewel around its neck. I think heaven must be more delightful than any place we might have here. Don't you think so?" I asked him.

"Yes, it must." He answered.

"Is the place where you live like heaven to you? Do you

love it?" I asked him as I started to eat my lunch.

"Yes, it is quite beautiful. I think you will be well pleased to live there." He said.

"I will miss my father and my brothers." I told him.

"Yes, I expect you will. We can visit them, and they can visit us if you like." He said.

"I'm sure the first time I say goodbye to them, it will break my heart. I suppose it is the difficult things in life that build character." I had tears forming in my eyes. I had to look away toward the window behind me as they fell down my cheeks. "Oh joy, the sun has come out in fullness today." I got up from my seat in an effort to hold back my sorrow.

Jacob was closest to me. He got up and put his arm around me to shelter me from view and secretly slipped me his napkin to wipe my tears.

"Jacob, I need some fresh air." I whispered.

"Father, Olivia is light-headed. I will take her outside for some air. We will be back in a moment." He said as he walked me outside. When we were out of their hearing and out of sight, I cried in his arms.

"My heart is breaking, Jacob. Father slapped my face and broke my heart. How can he insist that I marry a complete stranger? I can't even imagine it." I told him.

"How can I help you, Olivia?" Jacob asked.

"You can't. I love you, Jacob. I will miss you when I am taken away from here." I told him.

"You love Paul don't you, Olivia?" He asked.

"Yes." I answered.

"Tell Father. Paul has a good family. He is successful. Maybe Father will agree." Jacob suggested.

"No. Please, Jacob, promise me you will not mention it to Father. Give me your word." I begged him.

"Alright, Olivia. You have my word. Take your time; breathe." He said.

"It's time to put this plan in motion. Please ask Marvin to join me in the garden so that we can talk. Maybe he will walk away from me after he gets to know me better." I wiped my tears and forced myself to smile.

"We can hope." Jacob kissed me on the cheek before he left my side. Then he delivered the message to Marvin.

"Excuse me gentlemen, my bride awaits." He got up and pushed in his chair.

"How is she?" My father asked Jacob.

"Better in the fresh air." He answered.

"Thank you for lunch, Sir Douglas." Paul said.

"I'll walk you out, Paul." Charles offered. He walked Paul to the door. "Paul, if you love my sister, get her away from here. I promise to help behind the scenes as much as possible."

"I'm just waiting for her to let me know." Paul said.

Charles shook his hand. "Keep your eyes open for her

signal."

"I will, but I'm not making a move until she lets me know." Paul said. "If you need me, send for me."

"I will." Charles watched him leave.

Paul went to arrange for a minister to be available to him when he called and paid him a good deal of money for the inconvenience he would cause him.

I went to my bedroom early and locked my door. Then I waited until I was sure everyone was asleep. I took the key to my room and locked my door when I left. I made my way out to the fountain and found Paul waiting for me. He took me away without being noticed and directly to the minister. We were married immediately. Then he took me home to his parent's house and managed to get me into his room unnoticed.

"Olivia, you do know we have to sleep together and be together as husband and wife." He whispered.

"Yes." I whispered.

He took off my shoes and stockings. Then he helped me with my dress. "Olivia, just close your eyes and keep telling yourself that you love me, and I love you." He whispered.

I nodded yes. He realized how nervous I was, so he put his hands on my arms as my dress fell to the floor. "It will be fine Olivia. I promise. It's late, and you've already been through so much today. Let's just talk for a while." He whispered as he helped me into bed next to him. I only had my slip to wear as a nightgown.

I got comfortable in his arms and rested my head on his chest. "Talk to me about this part of marriage." I whispered.

"It might be easier if I just showed you." He suddenly heard his father snoring and realized how thin the walls were. "Or maybe talking would be a good thing." He whispered.

In the morning, we were resting in bed together when his father started banging on the bedroom door. "Paul! Get up. Charles is here. He says it is urgent."

"Send him up, Father." Paul said.

"What are you doing? My dress is on the floor." I told him.

"Trust me." He put on his pants. "One moment of embarrassment is worth a lifetime of not being harassed by your father. Just hold the blankets up against you and pull the straps of your slip off your shoulders completely. All I need him to see are your bare shoulders. A picture speaks a thousand words." Paul said. "Give him the impression you have nothing on. This is important."

"He is going to think something happened between us." I said.

"Olivia, we need him to believe that; otherwise your father can have our marriage annulled." He said.

Charles knocked on his door. "Paul, Olivia is missing. We need your help."

"Charles, before I open this door I want to warn you that I married your sister last night. I have the wedding rings and the marriage certificate signed. For her sake, stay calm." Paul waited for a reaction.

"Olivia?" Charles asked.

"Yes, Charles. We were married last night. I am Paul's wife in every sense." I told him.

"Open this door now!" He yelled.

Paul turned to me. "Don't get out of that bed no matter what happens and keep those blankets on."

I nodded yes as he opened the door.

My brother stared at me. "Did you?"

"Yes." I answered.

"Paul, a word outside." He said.

Paul winked at me and followed him out closing the door behind him.

"How did you arrange this? Give me the details." Charles asked.

Paul told him about the angel, the fountain, and the minister. "I love Olivia. You know I do, and she most definitely loves me. I will treat her well. I promise you." Paul told him.

"You may crush the deal on the wine." Charles warned him.

"Not right away. There is a temporary contract in place and your father won't risk his good reputation in business over this." Paul was confident.

"I'm happy for you. If anyone asks, I hit you and it hurt."

Charles said.

"Caught me by surprise." He smiled.

"Tell Olivia that her brothers will visit her no matter what our father decides." Charles held out his hand to Paul. "Welcome to the family."

"I'll let Olivia know." Paul said as he shook Charles' hand.

Charles knocked on the door. "I love you Olivia. Congratulations!"

"Thank you, Charles." I yelled back.

Charles left and returned to my family. Everyone gathered in the dining room. "Father, I found Olivia."

"Why didn't you bring her home?" My father asked.

"I'm sorry Marvin. Last night, she married Paul Stephens. I found her in his bed when I got there. The wedding rings are on their hands, and they have a marriage certificate. There is nothing we can do." Charles told him.

"Sir Douglas, you deceived both my father and me. We will not forget this. I insist you arrange for my transportation home immediately." He demanded.

"I'll take care of that for you." Keith escorted him out of the dining room.

"How could she do this to me, to us?" My father paced the floor.

"Father, didn't you slap her yesterday? You've never hit

Olivia before. She was heartbroken. She cried in my arms outside. She didn't want the marriage you arranged. She has a right to be happy. She apparently made her choice after you struck her." Jacob said.

"She didn't make up her mind then. She had this planned ahead of time. How did she know I was bringing Marvin here? Who told her?" He wanted to know.

"Paul did. He told her and the rest of us. Marvin was not a surprise to any of us." Charles told him.

"And the fainting? Was that an act?" He asked his sons.

"Olivia wanted to speak to you alone. That was the only way she thought it might happen." Keith told him.

"Did you conspire against me to have her marry Paul Stephens?" He asked.

"No, Father, none of us knew." Jacob told him.

"All of you are guilty of deceiving me with her." He yelled at them. "Get out! Get out!"

As my brothers left, they gathered up some of my clothes and sent them by messenger to Paul's home. Then they headed for the local tavern.

"Let's have a drink in celebration of our little sister's marriage to Paul Stephens." They raised their glasses together. "To Olivia Stephens. May she be happier than she has ever been and more prosperous than she could have imagined."

At the Stephens home, Mr. and Mrs. Stephens were informed by Paul that he had married me. He explained the unique circumstances that rushed us to the altar.

"Do you mean you brought your new wife into your bedroom, and we never knew it?" Mr. Stephens asked.

"Apparently, you are very heavy sleepers." Paul said.

Mr. Stephens smiled. "Now that you've accomplished your goal, what are your plans?"

"A special trip of course. I want to get her away from here." Paul said.

"Bring Olivia down to eat when she is ready." They invited him.

"About that. Olivia didn't have time to pack. She only has the one dress. Would you mind if I gave you her sizes and you did a little shopping for her? It's really too dangerous for her to be out today. Her father needs a chance to calm down."

"Run and get her sizes. We will leave the house for a few hours and get you both some wedding presents." Mr. Stephens told him.

He ran back to our bedroom. He asked me the specifics and wrote down the information. Then he ran back to them. "Thank you both." He rushed back into our bedroom and locked the door. "They will be gone soon, so we will have the privacy we didn't have last night." He jumped under the covers with me.

"Shouldn't we get up and get dressed?" I asked him.

"No, no, no, Olivia. I spent most of last night explaining the finer points of marriage to you." He wrapped his arms around me. "I can't have you believing that I am all talk."

"Aren't there rules about daylight?" I asked him.

"No, there are no rules about daylight." He laughed.

"Are there rules about eating first?" I asked him.

"Shssh." He put his hand over my mouth gently. "There are rules against wives trying to distract their husbands." He removed his hand and kissed me.

The butler knocked on the door and interrupted Paul's pursuit. "Sir, there is a messenger at the door with a package for your wife."

"Accept the package, and make sure no other person steps on to the second floor of this house for the next two hours." He yelled back.

"Yes, Sir." The answer came back.

We heard the scurrying of a few feet outside the door as the staff made their way to the staircase.

"Now, my dear wife, we have the privacy we need." He told me.

Chapter Six

Almost a week later, he broke the news to me that we were taking a trip together.

"Where?" I asked him.

"It is a surprise. Now pack your clothes and let's go. We have to be at our appointed place in an hour, and we cannot be late." He told me.

I was excited to go. His parents went with us to the harbor. They said goodbye and hugged each of us before we boarded the ship. They wished us a safe voyage as Paul grabbed our luggage. He handed me a small bag to carry.

"I've never been on a ship before." I told him.

"Come this way. I will show you where we are sleeping." He told me as we came aboard the ship.

We had a bed in a room. It looked comfortable and clean. There was just enough room to walk around it. There was a shelf beside it with a lantern hanging above. Paul put our luggage under the shelf.

"I haven't seen too many people on this ship." I told him.

"It is sort of a private venture. Our accommodations were

arranged in advance." He said as the ship sailed away from the harbor.

"By whom?" I asked him.

"I can't tell you yet." He answered.

"You can't tell me who paid for the trip and you can't tell me where we are going. What can you tell me?" I asked him.

"That I love you." He said as he attempted to kiss me.

"You are making me very nervous. I want to know where we are going." I insisted.

"France." He answered.

I was stunned. "France? You are taking me to France?"

"Yes. Surprise." He said softly.

"To meet your brothers and your relatives?" I asked him.

"Yes." He answered.

"Why didn't you tell me that before we left?" I asked him.

"I wanted to hold off as long as possible. I have a very big family." He said.

"I like big families. This is exciting." I told him.

Days later, we arrived at Marseille, a harbor near Paris. We departed the ship, and there was a carriage waiting for us. Paul loaded our luggage and helped me to get inside. The driver drove us a very long way to a beautiful mansion.

"Paul, your family must be very well off." I said.

"I would agree." He told me as the carriage stopped.

The door to the carriage was opened, and Paul stepped out. "Bring our luggage into the bedroom on the third floor at the right end of the hall." Paul ordered. Then he helped me out of the carriage.

"You've been here before." I remarked.

"Yes, Olivia." He took my hand. "Some people are waiting to meet you."

We walked into the mansion as someone from the staff opened the door.

"Come this way." He walked me into a formal sitting room. As we entered, two older gentlemen in suits stood up; and a woman about my father's age stood between them. "Olivia, I would like to introduce you to the Duchess Dupree."

I gasped and looked at him. I removed my hand from his and stood there facing her. I felt betrayed.

"Olivia, darling, I know this is a surprise to you." She said.

"Why am I here?" I asked her.

"These are the gentlemen who are guardians over your father's estate. They are here to verify that you are my daughter." She told me.

I backed up. "No, I'm not your daughter."

Paul quickly got behind me and held me in place. "Olivia, you know I love you. Please just listen."

"I don't know that at all." I told him.

"Please listen. The truth will make things right between us." He said to me.

Tears flowed down my cheeks. This was overwhelming.

"Years ago, you were taken from me. Your father Duke Dupree passed away, and you were the heir to his estate. We have been looking for you for years. You had a governess by the name of Charlene Yvonne a few years ago. She knew of our search for you. Two years ago, she wrote to me. In the letter she described the birthmark on your back. She told me your name and the name of your father. From that information I was able to verify who you were. I asked for Paul's help to find you and to bring you back to me. I promise you, Olivia, I can prove to you that you are my daughter. Just give me a chance." She was very soft spoken and sincere.

"I don't feel very well right now." I started to cry. "Could you excuse me please?"

"Certainly." She said.

"Paul, let go of me." I insisted.

He let go, and I walked out the front door. When I got to the bottom of the steps, I just started running. I didn't know where I was going. I wanted to get as far away from all of them as possible. Paul realized my intentions and chased me. He caught up to me and grabbed me by the arm to stop me.

"Olivia, let me explain." He begged.

I was crying. I fought to be free of him.

"Olivia, stop!" He held on tighter. Then he wrapped his arms around me like he was hugging me. He held me tightly against him until I gave up fighting and just cried. "Listen to me, please. I had to tell you all those things in the stable. You would not have trusted me if I had come against your father. I admit it was part of a plan to get you to marry me. I was deceitful and the lowest form of life. I admit it. I'm sorry I hurt you with those lies, but it was the only way to set you free from Sir Douglas and get you back to the life you were taken from. I do love you. I love you with my whole heart and breath and everything that is me. If you check our marriage certificate, you will find that our last name is not listed as Stephens. It is Chalon. You are Olivia Dupree Chalon. I am the Duke Paul Anton Chalon. This is my mansion, and Duchess Dupree is my guest. The ship we sailed on is my ship. The staff is my staff. Mr. and Mrs. Stephens work for me. Olivia please, if you understand the real truth about what has happened to you, I know you will find it in your heart to forgive me."

I pushed away from him and screamed at him. "Charles was right about you from the start. He said you were a liar and I shouldn't trust you. I fell for your charm and your lies. You are not even who you claimed to be. I loved you. I gave you me, not part of me, but all of me." I sat on the grass and cried. I couldn't stop.

"Please, Olivia, let me take you back inside. I promise we can sort this out." He said as he knelt down on one knee beside me.

"No, we can't." I wept. "You don't exist anymore. You died, and I am mourning the death of the person I loved."

"Olivia, don't say those things." It was breaking his heart to see me in so much emotional pain. Finally after an hour, he couldn't stand it any longer. "Olivia, I'm taking you back." He went to help me up and I refused his hand.

"I'm not going anywhere with you. Leave me here."

He couldn't believe that I could cry so much. "I'm not leaving my wife out here on the grass. Walk back with me, or I will carry you back."

"Leave me alone!" I yelled at him.

"I've had enough of this. The truth will heal your heart, and it will redeem me." He picked me up and I fought with him. He put me down on the grass. "You will cause me to hurt you if you keep kicking and scratching. Stop this now!"

"If you touch me, I shall fight with you as I would a criminal. Don't touch me!" I screamed at him.

"You give me no choice. I cannot leave you out here on the lawn. This is your last chance. Get up on your own, or I will carry you the only way you will allow me to." He threatened.

"I'm not going anywhere with you." I got up and ran from him again. He chased me down and held me by my arms. Then he yelled for his servant. "Bring me a rope and a knife."

"You would tie me? You are a beast!" I yelled at him.

"Then walk back with me." He refused to let go of my arms as I kicked his legs. "It's obvious you didn't need your brothers to protect you."

The servant came back with the rope.

Paul pulled me and forced me to lie down on the grass. "Tie her legs together."

"Sir?" The man was stunned by the order.

"Tie them!" Paul insisted.

"You are a beast! You are the lowest form of life! I hate you for betraying me! Do you hear me? I hate you!" I screamed at him.

He held my wrists together. "Tie her hands. I am done with being punched and scratched."

The servant did as he was ordered. Then Paul secured my hands by using the rope and wrapping it around my waist. Then he picked me up in his arms and carried me back into the mansion.

"Olivia, I cannot believe you would force me to do this to take you back into the house." He carried me up to our bedroom and put me on the bed. He untied the ropes. "You remember that you forced me to do this, Olivia. How dare you make me tie my own wife to get her to come into our home. I promise you the truth will heal your heart. I'll have someone bring you some food and something to drink." He left the bedroom and locked the door. He was afraid I was going to run away again.

The Duchess had witnessed what happened. "Dear sweet Paul, this must be breaking you heart." She said as he entered the sitting room.

"I should have found a way to tell her before we arrived here. This is my fault. If she doesn't listen to the truth and believe it, our marriage will never recover." He said.

"I can convince her just as I convinced you." She assured him.

"Duchess, we need to verify the birthmark. We can only stay here one more day." Mr. Baudin told her.

The Duchess looked at Paul for a commitment.

"I will make sure you see the birthmark tomorrow before you have to leave." He assured them.

They spoke about the evidence for an hour and verified pages of documents Paul's father had obtained over the years proving I was the daughter of the Duchess.

"If your father were alive today, I know we would have gotten her back sooner. To think Sir Douglas caused such sorrow by his selfish act of revenge. He is a horrible man." The Duchess was so frustrated by the current circumstances.

"Duchess Dupree, please be aware that Olivia loves the man. She has only known him as her father. If you speak ill of him, she will reject you." Paul warned her.

"Lord Duke, your wife refuses to eat or drink. She threw the food we brought her onto the floor and ordered us out of the room. I locked the door as you ordered." His maid told him.

"Make her another tray. Bring it to my room in twenty minutes." He told the maid. "Be prepared to clean up the mess that she made then."

"Yes, Lord Duke." She bowed and left.

"Excuse me please." Paul left his guests and came upstairs. He unlocked the door and stepped into the room. He saw me sitting on the floor in the corner of the room. "You look exhausted, Olivia." He came to kneel in front of me. "Let me help you into the bed so that you can rest."

"No thank you, Duke Chalon." I said softly.

"Olivia, all of this is unnecessary. If you will only listen to the truth, I am sure you will forgive me. Please give us all a chance to make this right."

"How do I get back home?" I asked him.

"Back to your father who hits you? Back to your life in a social prison? Do you remember what you left?" He asked me.

"Am I really better off here with you? A man who lies so easily and then ties his wife with rope? How are you better than my father?" I asked him.

"I admitted that I lied, but with the purpose of being able to repair the damage your father caused by stealing you in the first place. Olivia, you belong here. You are Olivia Dupree Chalon, the daughter of a Duke and Duchess. You have wealth and title. Sir Douglas stole years away from you. You have a mother who has cried for you for years. She never gave up looking for you; and here you are within arms reach after all those years, and you won't even allow her the gift of the simple touch of your hand in greeting. Are you going to force her to suffer at your hand too? Please come downstairs and just listen to the evidence. Don't make your mother suffer another day without you. Please, Olivia." He pleaded.

"I am a birthmark to her." I said.

"That is not true." He insisted.

I stood up and took off my dress and dropped my slip in front of him. "Call them. Call the guardians to look at my back. Get it over with so I can rest."

"I'm not letting other men come into this room and see my wife like this." He said.

"Fine, then I shall go to them." I walked toward the door defying him.

He picked me up and put me on the bed. "You will have what you want." He was angry and held me down to yell at me. "I have never in my life met such an unreasonable, stubborn woman. You defy all logic. I brought you here so that you could find out the truth about your life, and what have I received in return? You accuse me of betrayal when I am the one fighting for you. You cry until it makes you sick, and now you defy me as your husband and want to show the world your naked beauty. Olivia, I am at my end with you. This will go one way or the other. It is your choice, and don't think for a minute that I will not let you make it. If you want me to drag you downstairs and expose you to two strangers just as you are, just say the word and believe me that is exactly how it will happen. The shame will be completely your responsibility. However, if reason has somehow entered your mind, you will get off this bed and put on a robe. I will call the guardians of the estate into this room, and you will lean against me as I show them only the birthmark. You can hate me later for either choice, but you will hear the truth. Now choose!"

I knew he was serious. "The robe."

He let go of me and went to the closet. He got me a long robe and watched me put it on. Then he went to our bedroom door and told the servant standing outside to bring the Duchess and the guardians to our bedroom and to send someone immediately to clean up the mess I had made in the room.

He returned to me. "Olivia, come here and lean against me."

I didn't say anything. I put my head on his shoulder and he put one arm around my waist and moved the top of my robe so that the birthmark was showing. He moved my hair aside as I leaned against him.

There was a knock on our door.

"Come in." He invited them.

The Duchess was surprised to see me standing in a robe with my back to them and part of my back exposed.

"Gentlemen, take note of the proof you seek." Paul told them.

They looked at the birthmark.

"Duchess, we need to see the other one too." Mr. Baudin requested.

"What other one?" Paul asked.

"The one I never told anyone about until a few hours ago. I just told these gentlemen today." The Duchess said. "She has a scar on the back of her neck just above the hairline. It was made when Sir Douglas first tried to kidnap her from her crib. There was a fight for her, and one of the swords sliced the back of her neck. We need to lift her hair to see it. We will need to move some of her hair away from it to spot it."

"Olivia, we want the truth now. No one knew about this. I promise you. Don't move please." He let go of my waist and lifted my hair away from my neck. One of the men went to touch my hair. "Don't you dare touch my wife. I will have your hand cut off." Paul warned him. "Duchess, find the scar."

The Duchess started to cry as she moved the hair on the back of my head. I wasn't sure if I passed or failed the test.

"Thank you, Lady Olivia. Please forgive us. This is the last piece of proof that we require. You are most certainly the daughter of Duchess Dupree." Mr. Baudin said as the maid picked up the last of the mess in the room and carried it away.

I forced myself not to cry out loud, but Paul could feel my body start to shake as I made the effort.

"Please, all of you, leave us." Paul said. He rubbed my back. "I'm so sorry, Olivia. I know that your heart did not want to believe it. You needed the truth, and this was the only way to get it to you. If no one had mentioned the scar, we would have never noticed. It is so well hidden under your hair."

I moved away from him. "You should go. Certainly you do not want to be burdened with any more of my sorrow."

"That is not true." He said.

"Isn't it? Isn't that what you just told me a few minutes

ago?"

"Olivia, the tears I complained about were the ones that had no end. Those tears weakened you and hurt you physically. I didn't want you to suffer while you resisted the truth." He told me.

"I've lost all I have known. I loved my father, and you have revealed him to be a criminal and a manipulator. I loved my brothers, and now I have none. In a moment in time you have revealed a truth to me and ripped the people I love out of my heart and life. I lost five people and gained one mother in the process." I told him.

"Five?" He asked.

"My father, Charles, Keith, Jacob and you." I told him.

"You haven't lost me." He insisted.

"Yes, Paul, I have. You are a stranger to me. Your name is different. Your profession is different. The country you live in is different. Your loyalty is different. The manner in which you treat me is different. I have lost you."

"Olivia, we can find our way back to each other. Don't you think you needed to know the truth? Don't you think Duchess Dupree deserved to find the child who was taken from her? This was the only way I knew of to get you to the truth. Will you throw me away because of it?" He asked.

"You threw me away first." I told him.

"No, I did not." He approached me.

I backed away from him. "Please don't touch me again."

"Olivia, you don't mean that." He said.

"Please. Find me another bedroom without you."

"I won't do that. If you leave my side now while you are suffering so much emotionally, the fight to save our marriage will be harder." He said.

"I am not sleeping in your bed." I insisted.

"Olivia, I understand that you want someone to blame for all of this turmoil, but I am not the one to blame. I did not set you up for this. That was the doing of Sir Douglas. He is the one who took you away from your heritage. He is the one who kidnapped a baby away from her mother. He is the one who deceived you and your brothers for almost eighteen years. I didn't do anything except bring you the truth." He said.

"Stop it!" I yelled at him.

"No. Olivia, he set this up from the beginning. He was going to give you up to a stranger for his own gain. If you want to compare him to me, look at our motives. Look at our hearts. Open your eyes Olivia. The one who truly loves you is standing in front of you. You haven't lost me or your brothers. They will still love you. They are welcome here."

"Please go away." I begged him.

"I won't leave you. I love you. I won't accept your rejection of me. I love you too much to let you push me out of your life." He insisted as he approached me again.

I backed away from him until my back was against the wall.

"I love you, Olivia, and you know I do." He leaned his

forehead gently against mine as I put my hands on his chest to keep him away. He took my wrists as gently as possible with his hands and moved my hands off of his chest. "I love you, Olivia, and you know that I do."

He moved his lips toward mine and my heart remembered our love. I let him kiss me. It was like a wave passed over me. I didn't want to feel pain any more. I had felt so much of it since we arrived. I wanted us to be the way that we were and he wanted it too. He wasn't invested in a few moments of affection. He was invested in healing his wife and his marriage. He was gentle, affectionate, patient and loving. He spoke to me in whispers and touched my heart and soul in unfamiliar ways. Hours later, we were closer to each other and more in love than we had ever been. I was sure that he was someone I could always count on. I completely forgave what needed to be forgiven. Perfect love had cast out all fear.

We stayed together in each other's arms all through the night and into the afternoon of the next day. Paul had our meals brought to our room. He wasn't willing to let anyone invade our contentment with each other. At three o'clock, I asked him if I could see Duchess Dupree. I wanted to hear her story about what really happened. He agreed. He got dressed before me.

"Olivia, come downstairs when you are ready. I'll be waiting with the Duchess in the sitting room. If you change your mind, just tell one of the servants. We don't have to do this today." He told me.

I kissed him. "I'll be fine now. Don't worry." I watched him leave our room. I got dressed and joined them downstairs fifteen minutes later.

"Duchess, I'm not sure about all of this yet. I know you have waited to have your daughter returned to you. I understand about the birthmark and the scar that you have declared as proof of my heritage, but I am still uncertain about so many things. Please be patient a little longer with me." I told her.

"Yes, of course, Olivia. This has been a tremendous shock to you. I understand." She replied.

"Please explain it all. I need every detail. Do not spare my feelings, I beg you."

We sat across from each other. Paul held my hand while she spoke.

"Alright. Your father Duke Pierre Dupree was very close to King Henry. They spent a good amount of time together discussing politics and other things men discuss. During the time I was carrying you, rumors of rebellion reached the King's ears. He sought your father's help to discover the identity of those who would come against the rule of the King. Your father was completely loyal to King Henry. The investigation took longer than the King was willing to wait, so he used other methods to obtain his information. I heard stories of torture and horrendous hardships that our people had to endure for the sake of information. Your father was upset about innocent blood being spilled. It was his outspoken objection to the methods that were used that put him in the line of fire as a suspect.

On the night you were born, a young couple who had traveled from England to France were in need of a doctor.

Olivia's Story

They stayed here with Paul's father and mother. Sir Douglas was visiting Paul's father to discuss the wine. Sir Douglas left his wife for a night so that she could rest while he visited with other men in France. Luc Chalon, Paul's father, was entrusted to keep her safe and provide for her needs. I needed the doctor to help with my delivery of you. Duke Chalon arranged for a midwife for Mrs. Douglas, but she was ill equipped to handle the seriousness of her condition. Duke Chalon was aware of both situations and refused to pull the doctor away from me. Sir Douglas arrived and saw the great suffering of his wife. He feared he would lose her and he begged Duke Chalon to use his influence to pull the only doctor in the area away from me. He even begged for the location of our home, but in his troubled state the Duke feared for my safety. He refused him. Sir Douglas watched his wife die a painful death with their child still inside her. He was angry and full of grief. He threatened revenge. Paul's father apologized. He offered to take care of every expense. His sorrow was great for the loss, but he wouldn't give us over to Sir Douglas. He let Sir Douglas stay in the area until his wife was buried. Then he arranged to send him back to England. We thought he had gotten on the ship, but he managed to escape the Duke's watchful eye. A few weeks later, he came into your nursery and managed to remove you from your cradle. A servant startled him and screamed, and he cut her down. Your father went after him with a sword. In the battle you were grazed with the sword. Sir Douglas wounded your father, but he was run off leaving you behind. We prayed that would be the end of it as we attended your father's wound." She explained.

"Then how did he kidnap me?" I asked her.

"As your father was trying to recover from his injury, King Henry was convinced that your father had betrayed him. He gave orders for your father to be assassinated and all his property taken. Your father feared for our safety. He was too weak to flee with us. I kissed him one last time, and he kissed you knowing that in a short time, he would be dead. I left alone with you in my arms and fled the wrath of the King. I had money and distant friends in Poland who would take us in. I would be a woman alone with a child until I got there. I hadn't seen Sir Douglas. I didn't know what he looked like. He joined me on my journey to Poland. In a few short days he gained my confidence. He seemed so considerate and kind. I began to trust him with you. I put you into his arms so that I could arrange further passage for us. When I turned around, he was gone. He stole you from me. I lost your father, our estate, and my only daughter in less than two weeks. I was beyond frantic and heartbroken. I had no idea where to look for you."

"How awful that must have been for you." I said. "Is there more to tell?"

"Yes, Olivia, much more." Paul said as he held my hand. "Please continue Duchess."

"While I was in Poland, Duke Luc Chalon came to see me. He was a wonderfully strong individual with the same smile and attitude as Paul is blessed to carry. I told him my story, and he promised he had information that would clear my husband's name and restore my estate to me. He had to do that first before he could start looking for you. It took him only six months to prove that your father was forever loyal to King Henry and that he had been set up. My property was restored conditionally. I could have it under guardianship until I produced you as the only true heir your father had. Upon your eighteenth birthday, if I had not found you, all would be lost to us.

Olivia, we did not know where to find you. Sir Douglas moved around so much that he was hard to catch up with. Our break came when a governess by the name of Charlene Yvonne contacted me with a letter. She wrote of your birthmark and your birthday. We did not want to force you out of the environment you had become accustomed to. We believed we had time to convince you of your birth. Our hope was that you would come back to me willingly. We did not count on the protection Sir Douglas put in place for your life, and we certainly did not want to wound any of your brothers. Paul's father planned to get you to me sooner; but something changed his focus, and he wouldn't elaborate on it. I waited patiently for his help. Then he was taken ill two years ago and died. Paul took over the plans to rescue you and bring you back to me. He wrote to me about how lovely you were when he first saw you. I can understand why he fell in love with you so quickly. You are indeed beautiful. I see it in his eyes every time he looks at you that he is entirely captivated by your presence. He kept me informed about his plans. I can show you the letters he sent me. They will reveal to you the heart of the man you have married." She told me.

"I have a question." I said.

"Ask anything you wish." She answered.

"Do you know why my father, Sir Douglas, would insist that I marry Earl Thomas Yates' son, Marvin?" I asked her.

"Yes, I do. You are in the royal line for the throne of France through your father's linage. That gives you access to the castle by invitation. Earl Yates is in the linage of the King of England. His family seeks a diplomatic appointment and the favor of the King of England. You are the invitation to that appointment. His son is just as ambitious as he is. They would have used you in whichever way it suited their political aspirations. I am sure that Sir Douglas would have prospered financially had the marriage gone through. His story of having been your rescuer and not your kidnapper certainly would have been supported by the Earl. It was my word against his. The difference is that I had witnesses to the first kidnapping, those who stepped in to help your father rescue you. The scar at the back of your neck proves my story. Very few knew of it and your father ordered them never to tell anyone unless he or I personally requested it. That was very wise of him." She explained. "Olivia, the father you knew kept your name the same. I named you Olivia. I can show you the birth certificate. You are my daughter, Olivia Adriana Dupree, the only daughter of Pierre Dupree and Constance Juliette Dupree. I am your Mama."

I stood up and held out my arms to her. She stood up with tears in her eyes, and we embraced each other.

"I am so sorry you have suffered so much, Mama." I held on to her.

"I have longed for the day I would hold you close and hear you call me Mama." She started to cry. "We will not speak of my past sorrow. My tears today are for the joy in my heart. Today my daughter has been returned to me. We begin from here." She did not want to let go of me.

When we let go of each other, she wiped the tears from her cheeks. "God has blessed me today."

"Mama, I do not speak French." I admitted.

She laughed. "What you do not know we can teach you. Come sit with me, Olivia. Tell me of the life you had. Tell me of your brothers. Paul wrote to me that they were honorable men who protected you well."

"Yes, they were and they still are. I understand now that they are not really the brothers I thought I had, but they are the brothers of my heart. That will not change. I do not know how to settle my love for Sir Douglas yet. I do not wish to hate him."

"You are a sweet girl, Olivia. In time, God will help you with those issues. Do not worry about me. I do not feel betrayed by you or your feelings toward him. Work it out in your own heart; and if you wish to tell me, then tell me. If you wish to hold it secretly, then do that. I am just happy to have you here with me knowing that you are aware of the truth." She said.

"Will I have to sign any documents for your estate to be restored to you?" I asked her.

"No. The guardians will transfer the estate over to the care of your husband. He will manage it for us. Paul has allowed me to use the manor as my home. He already has plans to make it self-supporting." She told me. "You can trust him, Olivia. I have known his family for many years. They are all good people."

"What would have happened if I had married Marvin

Yates?" I asked her.

"He would have inherited the estate. He could have thrown me out of it or sold it. Once you are married, your husband makes the decisions on all matters. The only things we have control over are what they allow us to control. It is a reality that all women should understand. If you want to protect your properties should he die, there are only two ways to do that. He puts it in writing before his death that you will inherit and rule your own property, or you have a child." She explained. "That changes if you remarry. Men always inherit the property of their wives. It is the law."

Paul interrupted us. "Speaking of that." He called in two men I had not met before. "Olivia, this is Mr. Bourdeau and Mr. LaCasse. They have drawn up legal documents that state that upon my death, all properties will be owned and ruled by you, my wife. I do not want you to find yourself in the same position as Duchess Dupree." He put the papers in front of me on the table and handed me a quill pen and ink. "Sign there and there. Make sure you sign it Olivia Adriana Chalon."

I did as he instructed me to do. Then he took the papers and blew on them until the ink was dry. His name was already on the papers. He handed them to Mr. Bourdeau and Mr. LaCasse. They signed as witnesses and pressed a seal on the documents.

"Duke Chalon, put these in a safe place." Mr. Bourdeau instructed. "I have made notes to record this as an official document."

"Thank you, Gentlemen. My man servant will show you to the door." Paul told them as his servant escorted them away from us.

"That is quite a gesture of love and faith." I told him as I stood up in front of him.

"Is it?" He smiled.

"You are determined to win my heart, aren't you?" I asked him.

"In every way possible." He kissed me on the lips. "Excuse me, Duchess. Your daughter seems irresistible sometimes."

"I do understand." She said.

My mother stayed with us for the next few weeks. Then Paul agreed that I could visit with her for two days at Dupree manor. That is how he referred to it. It was a beautiful, comfortable place with elegant furniture and unique art work. The gardens were lovely. She took me through each room describing the history of the place. Then we walked the grounds and visited the stable. The scenery around it was just as lovely.

"Mama, why does that man follow us?" I asked her as we walked back toward the manor.

"Your husband insisted that you be guarded while you are with me. He is just being cautious. You have not noticed but there are actually three men looking after you." She told me as she pointed them out.

"No, I hadn't noticed. They do attempt to stay well hidden. It seems this is the life I've had ever since I can remember. You would think that I were the queen and not just some ordinary citizen." I told her.

"Olivia, you have never been ordinary." She smiled.

"I have not written to my brothers yet. I don't know what to tell them." I told her.

"You might choose the one who is not so attached to your father and explain it first to him. You could invite him to your home." She suggested.

"That would be Jacob. He was the first to offer help to me. He has no fear of being cast out by my family. He is forever loyal to his love and protection of me." I explained.

"Start with Jacob then. In your heart Olivia, your brothers are still your brothers. If I may speak of Sir Douglas for a moment?" She asked my permission.

"Yes Mama, do speak." I listened.

"Sir Douglas started off doing this out of evil intent. We are aware of that, but has he ever treated you as less than a dear beloved daughter?" She asked me as we walked.

"He has always been loving to me. He did strike me when I refused to marry the Earl's son Marvin. I had seen him take a stick to my brothers when they were younger. I never defied him like they did while I was growing up. I was afraid of punishment. I thought he might be angry with me when I objected to the marriage, but I never thought he would strike me. It broke my heart." I told her.

"Have you forgiven him for it?" She asked me.

"Forgiveness does not mean that you invite someone back

into your life to repeat the action. I have forgiven him, but I don't trust that his anger won't push him to repeat the offense. I don't want him near me, especially now." I told her.

"Forgiveness can be a difficult thing. I realized that when I had to apply it to my own personal situations, but forgiveness will move me out of the way of the hand of God. It restores the peace in my heart and replaces my anger. There have been many times that I tried to forgive Sir Douglas. My hurt and the anger caused by what he had done just crept back into my thoughts. I found myself trying to forgive again and again with no real success. Then a dear friend taught me the secret of true forgiveness. It is biblically real. I confessed to God that I did not have it in my heart to forgive Sir Douglas. Then I asked God to work out the forgiveness in me. The good Lord sent someone across my path after that and we discussed it. He said that as God has angels and goodness for us, equally so the devil has demons and evil intent for our lives. He told me to picture Sir Douglas as being manipulated by evil to steal my child. I was to picture him as a puppet in the hands of the devil. He asked me to forgive Sir Douglas by praying for him and praying against the evil which held him captive. Then he told me to recognize the devil as the true source of your kidnapping, for all evil originates with him. Once I recognized the real thief, I was able to demand a seven fold return for what was stolen. The devil owed me payment and he had to pay. Since that time Paul's father stepped into my life, and worked to restore my husband's reputation. With that came a return of this manor and the lands that went with it. Friends came to support me and help me in ways too numerous to list. Wealth and prosperity came to me. Royal connections were restored. I have the best group of people serving my needs in my home. Then you were restored to me and married a young man who is like a son to me already. Over and over again, payment was received because I chose to forgive and I recognized the puppet master was behind the evil deed. God always gives us a good formula to prosperity. It is so simple really and most people miss it because they have swallowed a lie. The lie tells them that if they hold on to unforgiveness, it will reap its own reward. That could not be further from the truth. It was important for me to forgive and get out of God's way. I was god in my own life by holding on to an unforgiving spirit. I will let God be God and I will find peace in being his child."

"Mama, are there men of God around here who know this and teach it?" I asked her.

"Paul does." She replied.

"I don't understand. I was talking about a priest or a pastor." I told her.

"Your husband took up the role of a minister years ago. When he was just eighteen, he had a desire in his heart to touch the heart of God. His father supported his dream and sent him to the seminary to learn. Paul got discouraged there. He found that it was an institution that removed the love and active power of God and exchanged it for man-made rules. He left the seminary and sought God on his own. It was an amazing journey for him personally. He would come and talk to me about his experiences and the little miracles that God blessed him with. He had such excitement in his eyes. He drew many people to find a closer relationship with Jesus, including me." She told me.

"All the time I've known him he has never mentioned God. I've never witnessed him praying or going to church. How can he be both men?" I asked her.

"About four years ago Paul met a very special woman. She was sweet and beautiful like you. He loved her. They shared the same love and connection to God. Together they were quite impressive. He planned to marry her. Her name was Marita Marques." She looked up to heaven as if she were imagining a beautiful romance.

"What happened to her?" I asked.

"She had an illness that drained her physically until she passed away. Paul prayed for her continually. He cried out to God and felt like he got no response. On the day of her death, he stopped his pursuit of God. His heart was broken. We considered it might be broken beyond repair. He started taking on dangerous assignments. He spent his time pushing himself physically and mentally. He kept his good character but walked away from his connection with God. I have only seen a glimmer of hope for his return to that relationship since he met you." She told me.

"He watches me pray sometimes. When I mention God he listens but rarely comments. He knows that I believe in God and that I have a relationship with God. He has not shown me a church in this area. I miss that." I told her.

"Come with me tomorrow. We can attend church if you like." She offered.

"I would like that very much." I smiled.

The evening was very peaceful. I slept well. In the morning we traveled a short distance to church. My mother introduced me to her friends and the pastor. They were happy for us. Many had questions that I did not want to answer. My mother told them that we had agreed to concentrate on what was ahead and not what was behind. They accepted that as a hint not to ask too many questions about how I happened to be there.

Later that afternoon, I said goodbye to my mother and traveled back under guard to return to our mansion. It was hard to believe as I looked over acres and acres of grapes growing on the vine that we owned such beauty. I managed to come into the manor unnoticed by my husband. I decided to look for him and not include the servants in my search. After looking in all the open rooms, I went into his office. Paul didn't seem like a person who would want an office. He wasn't there. I shut his office door and decided to do a little harmless snooping. I looked through the papers on his desk. I found paperwork on the wine business. I sat in his chair and looked through his desk drawers. It was interesting that he kept records on the servants. I read personal information about them. I was putting those papers back into his drawers when I accidently caused a few papers to fall off his desk. I got off the chair and on my knees to pick them up. It was then that I spotted a key secured to the underside of the desk. My curiosity took over. I removed it and looked at the desk to find a key hole that it might fit. I turned it in the lock of the side drawer and it opened. There was a small box with personal letters written from my father Sir Douglas to Paul's father. I stole the letters and put the box back in its place. Then I locked the drawer and secured the key. I was careful to make sure that everything looked untouched before I left. I checked the hall and made my way upstairs to our bedroom. I was going to start reading them at that time, but I heard Paul's footsteps as he started up the staircase. I rushed to put the letters in my bureau under my clothing. I was shutting the drawer when he entered the bedroom.

"Did you have an enjoyable time with your mother?" He asked me.

"Yes, I did." I smiled.

"What is going on?" He asked.

"Nothing." I answered.

"You look like you are hiding a secret from me. You look guilty. Have you done something you should not have done?" He asked.

"No, well, maybe yes." I said.

"Which is it?" He asked.

"I did go into your office and look through the papers on your desk. I hope you don't mind." I told him.

"No, I don't mind. Look at whatever you want. This is your house too. I have no secrets from you." He said as he started to change his clothes. "Do you like the desk? I found it yesterday in storage. It used to belong to my father. It is in very good condition for an old desk, so sturdy. I have been going through the drawers, but one drawer is locked. I have no idea where to find the key to it. I don't want to break the lock yet. I have the servants searching." Once he had changed his clothing he came to put his arms around me to kiss me. "I've missed you."

"Paul, what happened to the desk you had?" I stopped him from kissing me.

"Well that is an odd question. It was a fair piece of furniture but did not compare to my father's desk in quality. I moved it into storage. Do you want it? I could have the servants make you some kind of office in any of these rooms you wish to have. Just say the word." He was so cheerful about the offer. He went to kiss me again, but I stopped him. "Olivia, what is the matter? I've missed you greatly. Was I right about something being wrong? Is there trouble of some kind?"

"Maybe." I replied cautiously.

"Let's have it so that we can move on to more important matters like me loving you." He said.

"I was very curious about what you did in your office so I looked through the papers on your desk and then the papers in your drawers." I told him.

"Snooping were you?" He laughed. "You look so guilty. Really, Olivia, I don't mind."

"I found the key that opens the drawer." I told him.

His eyes lit up. "Really? Where was it?"

"Secured under the desk. I dropped some papers. When I got down to pick them up I spotted it under the desk. My curiosity took over, and I was compelled to open the drawer." I told him.

"Did you find body parts? Olivia, you look so serious. What is wrong?" He asked.

"There was a box full of letters. I took them to read them secretly away from you." I told him.

"Why would you do that? Did you suspect me of some cruel deed or of being unfaithful to you?" He asked.

"I feel so bad about suspecting you of hiding more from me. I know you told me that you would be honest; but when I saw the letters, I thought you lied to me again." I told him.

"What is in these letters you are hiding?" He asked.

"They are letters from my father Sir Douglas to your father. There are four of them." I told him.

He let go of me. "That can't be. My father never mentioned that he had any correspondence with Sir Douglas. Are the letters signed by your father's hand? Is his seal on them?"

I went into my bureau drawer and pulled them out. I handed them to him. "I haven't read any of them yet."

"Your life continues to be a mystery to us. We owe it to ourselves to read these letters. Come to the bed, and we will sort them by date and go through them together." He said.

We sat on our bed together, and he sorted them by date. He handed me the first one to read to him. *"To Duke Chalon. Thank you for the shipment of four bottles of your finest wine. I regret that at this time, I am unable to market the wine for you.*

This area has exploded with new wines, and to add one more brand to the list already available would only burden the market in our area. Maybe in the future we could do business together."

"It seems only to be a business letter. There is nothing personal about that one. Let's go on." Paul handed me the next one.

"Dear Duke Chalon. My wife and I are planning a trip to visit your vineyard and meet with you personally. She has been twisting my arm to consider importing your wine and marketing it. She adored the taste of the white wine especially. We should be arriving within a week's time. I do have other appointments in the area; however, we will be stopping at your home first. I am looking forward to meeting with you." I read.

"This seems completely innocent, Olivia. Here is the next one." He said.

"You read it. Paul, if it is all business, then why would your father lock the letters up and keep them all these years?" I asked him.

"I don't know." He opened the next letter and started reading. "Let's just read the content of the letter. We know they are all addressed to my father." He began reading. *"As I write this letter, I am angered at the treatment my wife received in your country. I left her in your care to watch over and protect her, but you betrayed my trust. Then when she needed the help, you refused her request and then my own. Your decision cost me my wife and child. I will not forget that. I swear on the air I breathe that each of you will suffer for robbing me of their presence. Make no mistake, one day I will come and take what is yours and feed it to the vultures."*

"Oh my, Paul, that is a fearful threat against your family." I remarked.

"I think it is a good thing you found these letters. His marketing of our wines could destroy our reputation. I have to pull them from his hand." He told me.

"What of you and your brothers. The baby he lost was his youngest child. Would he go after you or your brothers?" I feared for their lives.

"Some things seem to make sense now after all these years. Let's read the other letter. I have questions that need to be answered." He said as he pulled the next one from the envelope. "It was written ten years later." He began to read. *"I knew it was only a matter of time before you discovered what I have done. I have made good on my threat to both you and your friend the Duchess. I lost one child and gained two. My hope is that each day you suffer in sorrow at your loss knowing that you could have prevented it by one decision years ago. You will not find us. I promise you that. Just like I have done in the past, I shall kill each one who attempts to take the substance of my revenge from me. If your pursuit to take back what I have stolen from you does not end then surely the empty grave you have will not be empty any longer. If you want life to be granted, then back off now or they will both suffer for your persistence. I always make good on my threats."*

"Oh, dear God!" Paul got up from the bed. "Could he have taken my brother too?"

"I don't understand." I watched him pace.

"I had a younger brother. He was two years younger than me. He disappeared. My parents searched everywhere for him. My mother was beside herself with grief. My father told us that he was found drown in the lake. He refused to show my mother the body. He told her he didn't want her to remember him that way. He had a coffin built and buried him on the property with a head stone. I have to dig up the grave. If it is empty, then my brother is your brother Keith."

"Wouldn't Keith have remembered he was taken?" I asked him.

"He was barely four years old when he disappeared." He explained. "His name was Collin."

I started to cry. "Paul, I don't want to know any more. I can't bear to know he is so evil." I got up from the bed.

"Olivia, we will put this to rest now. I will do what I must and keep you out of it as long as you like. I need to know the mind of Sir Douglas so I can protect you." He collected the letters from the bed and put them in his bureau. Then he returned to me and held me close to him.

"I don't want to be like this. I don't want to spend my life in sorrow and grief." I told him.

"I know you don't. This is a sad thing for you. Try to concentrate on us and our life here away from him. I promise to keep you safe and not in prison. You deserve freedom and fun. I shall make sure you have it."

I kissed him. "You are so wonderful to me even in the midst of your own questions and circumstances."

"I have a lifetime of love for you, and of course, our little ones." He patted my stomach. "No question is more important than you are to me. I shall sort this out."

"I love the way you are with me. There is no little one yet." He caused me to smile as I moved his hand from my stomach.

He moved his hand onto my stomach again. "There will be. I am a man who loves the art of creation. I shall make you a child that is more handsome than any other." He told me.

"And if it is a girl?" I asked.

"She shall look just like her mother. I decree it, for there is no one more beautiful than you." He touched me once again by his words. Then he held me in his arms and kissed me.

"You are a poet." I told him as we stood in each other's arms.

"Poet or not, we are expecting company." He took my hand and kissed it. "I will take care of all the things you don't need to worry about."

"Who is coming?" I asked him.

"My mother. She arrives in an hour. We will not mention any of this to her." He insisted.

"No, of course not." I agreed. "Paul, I am a mess. She will be disappointed in me."

"Never." He declared. "Take your time, and do what you usually do to yourself. Then come downstairs to join me. I have the servants preparing a meal for her arrival. You do not have to hurry. I have things to attend to first."

"I'm worried about meeting her. She doesn't know you are married." I reminded him.

"I will get her drunk on wine, and she will be as congenial as ever." He joked.

I laughed. "Be nice."

"I'm always nice to the people I love." He kissed me on the cheek. "Get ready. I'll be waiting for you downstairs." He went downstairs and talked to two of the men he trusted on his staff. "Tonight after it gets dark, you two will go to my brother Collin's grave and dig it up. When you have reached the coffin, you will pull it up and send for me. Not a word about this to anyone, not now and not ever."

"Yes, Sir." They agreed.

"I have grown to trust you both. I will reward your silence only once, but I will reward it." He promised.

"Thank you, Lord Duke." They both replied.

I joined him just before his mother arrived. We went outside to meet her carriage as it pulled up in front of the mansion. Paul insisted on opening the door for her and helping her out.

"Paul, you look wonderful." She smiled.

He greeted her with a hug. "I should. I have married the woman of my heart."

"Is this the woman of your heart?" His mother asked as she looked at me.

"Yes, Mother." He escorted his mother to me. "Mother, this is my wife, Olivia Adriana Dupree Chalon."

His mother gasped. "The daughter of Duchess Dupree?"

"Yes." He answered.

"Oh, my dear, I am so thrilled to meet you. You are lovely and so young." She said.

I smiled. "It is a pleasure to meet you. I have no idea how to address you."

She laughed. "You're adorable. Lady Jacqueline is fine for now. Shall we go inside? I think I would like to know about this story of love and how my son happened to decide to marry you. I am thoroughly disappointed that I was not included to look on when you said your vows."

Paul took my hand as his mother walked in front of us. "Don't worry. Let me explain it to her." He whispered. Then he turned to the servant at the door. "Carry my mother's luggage to her room on the second floor."

His mother removed her gloves and put them on the table as we walked into the sitting room. She sat down and made herself comfortable. "I am anxious for an explanation, Paul."

He kissed me on the cheek and then had me sit next to him. He never let go of my hand. "I took up the mission my father had to find Olivia and return her to the Duchess. I went to England and employed two people to act as my parents. We found Olivia at a celebration. She was guarded by her older brother Charles Douglas. The moment I saw her, I was in love. You will find her to be endearing in so many ways. It took some effort, but I managed to convince her of my love and gain the trust of her brothers. We didn't have very long together. Sir Douglas guarded her life; and when he was away her brothers took over that assignment. A few weeks ago, Sir Douglas arranged a marriage for Olivia. He was going to marry her off to the son of Earl Thomas Yates. Marvin Yates showed up at her home expecting a welcome from her. He was surprised when that did not happen. Sir Douglas was determined to have that marriage take place, and he physically assaulted Olivia to force her to comply. I knew she loved me. We had set up a signal between us. When she gave me that signal, I met her that same evening and took her away from them. We were married immediately so that Sir Douglas would not be able to get her back. That is why you were not invited to our wedding. I have had my bride in my arms for only a few weeks."

"Do you know your heart, Olivia? Are you sure you love my son?" She asked.

"I am naïve about love in general. I have been under lock and key the majority of my life. When Paul first told me of his affection toward me, I admit I wanted time to discover what attention and affection from men would be like. Not that I planned on committing myself as I would in a marriage. He understood my needs and agreed that was best. When my father presented me with Marvin Yates as a suitable husband, there was no comparison. I realized how elevated Paul had become in my mind and heart. I no longer wanted the attention or the affection of another man. Your son is gentle and kind in many ways. Even though we have had a few battles in this short time, he refuses to leave my side and his efforts always speak to my heart. I could love no other, Lady

Jacqueline."

"I told you she was endearing." Paul kissed me on the cheek.

"Very much so." His mother agreed. "Well, your explanation makes sense to me. I am not entirely hurt by missing my own son's wedding; however, I insist on a celebration of some kind to announce your wedding to society. I do not want Olivia hidden away in the shadows. We are proud to have her as a member of our family, and we should show our friends the wife you have been blessed with. I insist."

"Mother, we won't be doing that right away. This is a complicated situation. Sir Douglas is not aware yet that Olivia has been returned to Duchess Dupree. He has no idea who she really married. There will be no celebration until I am sure that my wife is safe from his hand." Paul told her.

"Who does he think you are?" She asked him.

"He thinks I am Paul Stephens, the son of Trevor Stephens. He was the man I hired to appear as my father. Until I move him safely away from Sir Douglas, I cannot risk a celebration of my marriage. If Sir Douglas finds out he was deceived, he will seek revenge against Mr. and Mrs. Stephens. They will be moving in a week. After that happens and I remove his hands from marketing and selling our wine, then maybe we can celebrate." He told her.

"This whole thing is disturbing. I am weary from my trip. I will be in my room resting for a while. We can discuss this later." She told him.

"Mother, I have moved all your things to the second floor. Your room is to the left of the staircase. I have taken over the third floor entirely." He explained.

"As you wish." She kissed him on the cheek and went up the staircase.

"Is she upset?" I asked him.

"It's hard to tell with my mother. She has very subtle ways while she is thinking about things. Should she reach some kind of decision, there will be no question about her feelings. I believe she will treat you well, Olivia. If there seems to be any sort of friction, please talk to me about it." He suggested.

"I will, but if I believe I should address it, I won't wait for your approval." I told him.

"In that case, I trust you will find a way to work it out with my mother without involving me. If you choose to wait and speak to me about it first, then I will be happy to help you handle it or handle it for you." He said.

"You are such a diplomat." I remarked. "Paul, your mother will miss the special lunch you had prepared for her."

"No, she won't. I thought about this first meeting, and I delayed it for an hour. We will sit with her then." He assured me.

"Paul, do you remember telling me that you would explain to me about your relationship with God? You never did get around to that." I reminded him.

"Duchess Dupree filled you in, didn't she?" He asked.

"On some things." I admitted.

"Come with me." He took me past the garden and up to the tree line. There were three headstones surrounded by flowers. I read the names and the dates. He pointed to Marita's. "I never thought I could love anyone as much as I loved her. She was my soulmate. She had big beautiful brown eyes like you and a smile that would melt me into a puddle. Her laugh was amazing. I think we actually shared the same thoughts sometimes. She was so connected to God. We would sit for hours talking and lose track of time. She loved God, and I was right beside her believing in Him with everything I had in me."

I was bothered by his explanation. I felt for the first time that I didn't have his heart as he stared at her headstone. He finally noticed the effect his words were having on me.

"Olivia, please let me finish before you judge us." He took me to sit with him on the grass. "Marita became very ill. She was weak and lost so much weight she looked like bones with skin. I prayed for her. I prayed for her night and day. I went to church and cried out in the night for God to save her. I believed up until her last breath that he was going to turn this around and give her back to me. Even as she died I believed he would raise her up. I believed and they buried her. The only person in my life at the time, that my heart truly wanted, was her. She was so good and suddenly she was gone. I became so angry with God that the people who knew me didn't even recognize me. I walked away from Him. I walked away from my belief in anything that had happened before that day. Every moment that I had known Him seemed an illusion. Every miracle prior to her death that I had experienced became ash. I refused to believe that any of it was real. Many people tried to talk to me, but I was so angry and disappointed about losing her. God let me go on like that. He let me walk out my own choice. Then when my father was dying, he asked me to find you. It was a father's dying wish to his son. He could have chosen Philippe or Andre, but he didn't even mention it to them. He told me to find you and bring you back to the Duchess. He said it meant more to him than any other thing in this life. He promised me that all the answers to all the questions of my heart would be settled when I had fulfilled his dying wish. How could I refuse him? I promised him that I would find you and bring you back."

"Have your questions been answered?" I asked him.

"More than you realize. I loved Marita, and I still love the memory of her in the time that we shared. I cannot put that aside. It is part of me. When I love, I love deeply. It is just who I am. Olivia, the memory of Marita does not even come close to the reality of you. Everything that she was to my heart fades in your presence. I can speak of her the way I did because simple words will describe her, but words do not describe you. You are air to me. I know I would die without you in my life. I don't believe God took Marita away from me. I see now that God graciously came to get her when death thought it had won. He reached down at the moment when death thought it had triumphed, and He lifted her to heaven to be like an angel beside Him. I always looked at the death instead of the life ahead for her. She is on streets paved with gold. She is in His presence for all of eternity. What better gift is there for a daughter of the living God? My anger was misdirected. I didn't see the journey ahead. Had I gotten my way, we would not be together. I would have missed God's best for me. I watch you pray, and I say nothing. I hear you speak about God, and I have no comment. It isn't out of indifference that I do this. It is out of awe for Him who gave you to me. I am speechless in His presence. You are the answer to the questions of my heart; and each day, I get another answer. I love you, Olivia. There is no one else."

His words brought tears to my eyes, and he thought even that was a precious gift to him. He kissed me sweetly on the lips and took my hand to lift me to my feet.

"From now on, I will do my best to be the man God had faith in me to be. I do not want to disappoint you. We will pray together and I promise to pray for you. I will look for a church for us. If I can't find one that is a witness to our hearts, then you and I will be a church together with the children we will have until God provides the right one for us." He promised me as we walked back toward the mansion.

Chapter Seven

One month after Paul discovered that the coffin of his brother was empty, he decided we had to start planning for the future. He believed a confrontation with Sir Douglas was eminent.

Mr. and Mrs. Stephens moved away from Sir Douglas. Paul managed to cancel his wine contract with him. He was careful not to reveal his true identity and enlisted the help of his brothers Andre and Philippe.

Then he wrote to Charles asking him to soften the heart of Sir Douglas toward our marriage. He told Charles of our love for each other and how happy I was to be among his family in France. He asked Charles to use discretion and not to reveal the letter or the address from which it was sent.

Charles wrote back that his father was still angry beyond words about the marriage and viewed me as the daughter who had betrayed him. He was so angry in fact that he barely spoke to Jacob in a civil tone because of his defense of my actions. He wrote that his father spent much more time with Keith, granting him the favor and wealth that he had never had access to before.

I sent a letter to Charles and asked him to keep it sealed and give it to Jacob when Father wasn't around. Charles was happy to do that. I invited Jacob to come to France to live with us. Paul thought it would be a better atmosphere for him, and he knew that I missed him.

Jacob replied that he was packing that very day. He explained that he had his fill of Father's wrath, and it was time to get out on his own. He promised not to be a burden to us and to find his own place as soon as he could find employment. We got the letter one day before he arrived. He was surprised when the driver of his carriage pulled up in front of our mansion.

I saw him from the third floor window and ran down to meet him grabbing Paul on my way. We opened the door as he was about to knock. I jumped into his arms.

"Jacob! I have missed you so much!" I told him as I squeezed him tightly around the neck.

"I can tell." He smiled at Paul as he hugged me. "Seems you've put on a little weight sister."

"Oh my, what a horrid thing to say." I let go of him.

He laughed. "I was kidding. You look and feel wonderful. What is this place?" He asked as we invited him inside.

"Paul owns it." I told him.

"He does?" He looked around astonished at the elegance and size of our home. "And the vineyards I passed?"

"Mine too." Paul told him.

"Really? I seem to be at a loss here. I thought you were just a seller of wine." Jacob said as one of the servants took his things.

"Put his things on the second floor in the guest bedroom." Paul instructed the servant. "Make sure everything is fresh and clean."

"Come sit with us Jacob. We have a lot to talk about." I took his hand and brought him into the sitting room.

"We've been keeping in touch with Charles. He has told us about Sir Douglas and the family. Olivia and I thought it was a wonderful idea to get you out from under all of that. We are sorry we caused you so much trouble." Paul told him.

"My father has wanted his own way for years. When we were younger, it wasn't so bad. This past year, however, his personality changed so greatly. I never thought I would see the day he would strike Olivia. Since you left with Olivia, he has been an absolutely unreasonable person to me. Charles he only sees at work and Keith is his new found project. It is like we are opposite sides of a coin. I've never seen so much favor on Keith's life from my father's hand. I don't understand it. He keeps talking to him about tracking down his heritage and finding his people. How can he imagine that he would be able to find the family of a street urchin?" Jacob explained. "Olivia, I am so sorry. I rambled on without regard for you. You didn't know about Keith. We kept it from you at Father's request."

"I know about Keith." I told him.

"How did you find out? Did Charles tell you?" He asked.

"No, I found a letter written by the hand of Sir Douglas to

Paul's father years ago." I told him.

"I've never heard you call our father Sir Douglas. Why do you refer to him that way now? No matter what he has done, he is still our father." Jacob insisted.

"Jacob, do you love me?" I asked him.

"Of course I do. You know I do." He said.

"You knew all along that Keith was not the natural born son of your father. Did you ever suspect that about me?" I asked him.

"You? Of course not. He brought you home in his arms. I don't understand why you would ask me that question." He replied.

"I'm not the natural daughter of Sir Douglas. I have obtained proof beyond any doubt." I told him.

"It can't be true. You have been with us since your birth. Father brought you home wrapped in a blanket and told us that Mother died giving birth to you. What is this evidence and to whom do you think you belong now?" He asked.

"Jacob, this is a letter written by your father's hand to my father. You know your father's seal and his handwriting. Just read it." Paul handed it to him.

Jacob examined the broken seal. He was very familiar with his father's handwriting. He sat quietly and read the short letter. "Is there more?" He asked.

Paul handed him the next letter written ten years later.

"Good grief, this is awful!" He looked up at me. "Did you know about all of this Paul before you came to meet us?"

"No, not all of it. Olivia discovered the letters in an old desk my father had years ago. They were locked away and she was curious and discovered the key to the desk drawer. She opened it and found the letters tucked away in a box." Paul explained.

"What did you know when you came?" Jacob asked him.

"I am a friend of Duchess Dupree. I've known her for years. My father vowed to help her find Olivia and return her. He slowed down his efforts after he was sure Sir Douglas kidnapped my younger brother Collin or as you know him now, Keith. I believe he couldn't risk Sir Douglas carrying out his threat to kill Collin. I believe he feared for Olivia's life as well. There is so much my brothers and I have been checking into since we discovered the letters. On my father's death bed he asked me to promise to find Olivia and return her to the Duchess. My father never told me about Keith. I would not have known if Olivia hadn't stumbled across those letters. I love Olivia. I can assure you that your sister loves me. We have a wonderful life here. I have wealth as you can see. You are a precious brother to us. The circumstances don't change our heart toward you. You are our family."

"This explains so much about the things I did not understand growing up. You were a purse to him, just like Keith is now. He wanted to cash you in and now he will try to do the same thing to Keith. Father doesn't know any of this has been revealed to you, does he?" He asked.

"No. We've not contacted him with the information. He

only knows Paul as Paul Stephens, not Duke Paul Chalon. He still believes I am Olivia Stephens and that I don't know my connection to Duchess Dupree." I told him.

"You do realize that my father is going to bring Keith right up to your doorstep to claim some kind of inheritance. He will want his share of it and Keith's good favor." Jacob said.

"We do believe that will happen. We have heard rumors that Sir Douglas has been inquiring about my father's death. He does not know my father kept the letters. We believe he will claim a good deed done and want a reward for returning my brother." Paul told him.

"How could Father prove he was Collin? One boy looks just like another." Jacob said.

"Not in this family." Paul rolled up his sleeve and exposed the top of his arm. "Royals are very particular about protecting their heritage. Every child born in the family line of Chalon carries this mark on their body in this exact place. It starts out small; but as we grow, it grows with us. There is no way to duplicate it as it is worn into the skin. A close examination of this mark would reveal Keith as my brother Collin. Olivia told me that she has seen the mark."

"I have too. Everyone in our family has seen it." Jacob told him.

"Some Royals depend on records of birthmarks. That is how I was identified to the guardians of the Dupree estate and to my very own mother." I told Jacob.

"I feel like I should check myself over. Maybe I was

kidnapped too." Jacob said.

Paul smiled. "I know this is a shock to you, Jacob."

"Ah, well, what can I do about it? I'm not giving up my sister or my family. I feel sorry for my father even though he doesn't deserve my pity. What he did was wrong beyond imagination, but I still don't want what he is headed for to happen. Is there mercy somewhere in this plan? I know you have a plan. You are too smart, Paul, not to have a plan." Jacob said.

"I feel like we have to wait until he makes a move with Keith. Until then, all of this has to remain a secret to him." He gestured as he was referring to the mansion and their current station in life. "All we can do is prepare for that day. You can help me by filling in any information I might need that Olivia would not have access to."

"I am in this to help my sister and my brother. I don't care about their original source of life. I care that they are still my brother and sister in my heart. Nothing has changed for me in that regard. As far as my father is concerned, just let him walk away from this with his life. Give him the chance to repent before God before he dies. That is all I ask. Every other payment he has to make to make this right, I support." Jacob said.

"I promise you Jacob, I will not take his life. However, if he threatens to kill my wife or my brother I will not keep that promise." Paul told him.

"I understand." Jacob stood up. "It has been a long journey and certainly an emotional surprise for me. Can you show me to my room, Olivia? I would like to refresh myself and change out of these clothes."

I took his hand. "Come with me." I walked with him up to his room.

"So this is all yours. Very nice indeed." He said as we climbed the staircase.

I opened the door to his bedroom. "I hope you like it."

"I am overwhelmed. I feel like the King's son." He replied as he walked in with me.

"I can have the servants draw you a bath if you like?" I asked him.

He smelled under his arms. "No, I'm good." He smiled.

I laughed. "I'm so glad you are here with us. Jacob, Paul's mother, Lady Jacqueline, lives here with us. She has the room on the other side of the staircase. She is very proper and French. She speaks English very well, but she prefers French. She is in the garden area, reading. Be careful not to startle her."

"Did you know that I understand French? I can't speak it very well, but I understand it most of the time." He told me.

"Really? You never told me that." I was surprised.

"Let's keep it between us. I had a few friends who got in trouble many times. The conversations their mothers would have with them and about them were hilarious. I will be your ears if you don't understand something. It will be like the old days at home. We will use our own secret code. Did you ever tell Paul that we had that between us?" He asked.

"No. We haven't used that code in years." I reminded him.

"Well then, let's take a few minutes later and brush up on it. Keith knows it too. You were away, and I was bored without you so I taught him." He informed me. "Olivia, be aware, as much as Keith is enjoying the favor and wealth of our father.... I'm sorry. I mean my father. He suspects something is going on too. He told me himself that he doesn't trust Father's motives."

"Should we write to him?" I asked.

"Let's talk to Paul about that first." He suggested.

"How did you leave?" I asked.

"I told Charles and Keith that I was leaving to visit you and that I would be in touch through Charles. I think it is very wise not to send any correspondence to our home." Jacob said.

"Jacob, it is confusing to me too. Don't correct yourself so often. It will work itself out eventually. What about Father? How did you tell him you were leaving?" I asked.

"I had Keith tell him. I was sure if he were upset about it, he would not be upset with Keith. Any contact with him since you left has been unbearable. I'm sure he was not surprised that I left the house without telling him." Jacob said.

"What did you say to him that made him so angry?" I asked.

"I was angry with him for striking you. I told him that again when I got back from drinking with Charles and Keith. We were celebrating your successful marriage to Paul at the tavern. He was still angry and ranting about you. I was uninhibited so I told him exactly how I felt. I told him that only a coward would strike a woman. He responded to my comment with his fists. Keith pulled him off me. It was all down hill after that." Jacob explained.

"I'm so sorry." I said.

"Don't be. It was the first time in my life, drunk or not, that I felt proud of myself in his presence. I may have deserved the beating because he is my father and my language was from the gutter, but I'm not sorry I said it. If he wasn't my father I would have gone after him after you cried in my arms. You know I love you dearly, Olivia. You and I have always had a special bond as brother and sister. I won't let anyone hurt you again." He promised.

I hugged him. "I love you too. You freshen up. If you get hungry and I'm not around, just go into the kitchen and ask someone to make you something to eat. The people who work for us are very nice. Amelia speaks English. Ask for her."

"Do the servants live here?" He asked me.

"Some do and some don't." I answered as I shut his door to give him privacy.

He walked down to the kitchen later and entered as the help was busy preparing chickens for supper. They were surprised by him and looked up.

"Amelia?" He asked.

She stood up and accidently hit a cup of flour on her way

spilling some on her face. She tried to wipe it off as the others laughed. She smiled as Jacob laughed too.

"I'm sorry." He apologized.

"No, no, it's alright. I do look ridiculous." She agreed.

"And beautiful." Jacob said.

"Yes, that too." She smiled. "How can I help you, Sir?"

"Please call me Jacob. I was told that if I were hungry, I should come to the kitchen and request something to eat. Olivia told me to ask for you." He said.

"Follow me, Jacob." She took a cloth and wiped the flour from her face and hands. Then she led him to the hallway behind the working kitchen. "We have bowls of fruit here and trays of pastries. If you would like bread with cheese or meat I can put that together for you. Just tell me what you like and I will make you a plate."

"Bread, meat and cheese would be a nice start with something to drink. Maybe an apple too." He said.

"Where would you like me to bring it?" She asked him.

"I haven't had the tour of the mansion yet. Where would you suggest I eat it?" He asked her.

"The dining room or at the table near the garden. They are both very comfortable and nice places to eat." She said.

"And where could I eat it and enjoy your company too?" He asked.

"I am afraid that won't be possible. My work day is not over for a few hours, and I'm sure your station in this life is well above my own." She replied.

"I have no station. I am simply important by association." He told her.

"Jacob, I know my place. If I sit with you, others will talk badly about me as if I were trying to elevate my position in life by getting your attention. I think we should leave well enough alone. I will make your plate. You will be grateful. I will smile and you will smile. Then I will go back to work. Please pick the place you want to eat." She told him.

"One question first." He persisted.

She laughed. "Yes?"

"Are you involved with another man?" He asked.

"No. There is no man worthy of my time." She replied.

He loved her personality. "I will be at the table near the garden. Thank you, Amelia."

She walked one way and he walked the other. A few minutes later she brought him out his plate of food and the drink. "When you are done, just leave the plate and glass here. I will come back for it." She turned to walk away and he gently grabbed her hand.

"Amelia, I'm not giving up on you." He said.

She removed her hand gently. "You will." Then she left.

I saw what happened when I was coming to join him. I sat

down next to him. "She is beautiful, isn't she?"

"Yes. Olivia, what is the story with her? She won't give me the time of day." He asked.

"She works for us. I noticed there is a lot more gossip that goes on around here. Even though I don't really understand the language, it seems the tone of the conversations reflect that everyone has an opinion about someone. In some ways, I am glad I do not understand it. Amelia is very smart. She is young, but she runs the kitchen. All those people doing what they do answer to her. She is a genius with food. She is not the cook, but she could be. Her organizational and people skills are amazing. She can read people. She probably had you figured out in thirty seconds." I told him.

"Can you elevate her station in life by her job?" He asked.

"I'm not sure what the customs are here, but I could ask Paul. Why do you ask?" I offered.

"Isn't it obvious? I want to get to know her better. Until she sees us as equals, she won't give me that chance." Jacob explained.

"Well the other option is lowering your station in life to meet hers." I smiled.

"You know what? That isn't a bad idea at all. I need a job here. I can't be living off of Paul's generous spirit forever. Can you see if you can give us a job equal to each other without lowering my importance to you too much? Just look into giving her an opportunity to rise up a bit." He suggested.

"I'll mention it." I promised.

Chapter Eight

Paul invited a gathering of nobility to our home, including my mother, Duchess Constance Dupree. He thought it was time to announce our marriage to them. I was very nervous about it, but he assured me that each of the people invited was discreet and would respect our privacy.

Jacob was now Paul's personal assistant, and Amelia was now mine. They stood behind us as we entered the room.

"You arranged this, didn't you?" She whispered to Jacob.

"It makes sense. My sister does not speak or understand French. You understand English and French and speak both well. This job makes us equals." He whispered back.

"You are smarter than you look." She remarked quietly.

He smiled. "Then I must be a genius."

Amelia had to find a place away from us to laugh. She hid around the corner and covered her mouth while she laughed at his remark. He knew what she was doing, and it amused him. She came out and shook her finger at him to warn him away from her. Jacob shook his head no.

"Amelia, accompany me." I whispered to her.

"Yes, Duchess." She followed me into the room and translated conversations to me that I did not understand. I answered in English, and she would translate back to the person I was speaking with in French. I loved having her by my side.

Jacob stayed close to Paul. Paul introduced him as Jacob Douglas, a close relative and his right hand man. Everyone was very nice. Jacob understood the French, and he could answer simple yes or no questions; but the more detailed conversations were left up to Paul.

My mother and Paul's mother got along very well with each other and the other women in the room.

"Paul, you might have a bit of trouble." Jacob warned him.

Paul turned toward him. "Be specific."

"You have three women in the corner talking about how the countryside will be shocked to learn that the daughter of the Duchess has been found and returned to her. They also mentioned Olivia's age and your prominence. There is jealousy and gossip going on over there. If you don't nip it in the bud, it will ruin you and endanger Olivia." Jacob warned him.

Paul walked directly over to the ladies. "Good evening ladies. My apologies for not speaking with you sooner."

"Duke Chalon, we realize how busy you are. We are honored that you included us in your invitations." Mrs. Delores told him.

"I only invited people of high character to this gathering. It was and still is important to me not to invite gossips and those who would endanger my wife by sharing the news that she has been returned to her mother, the Duchess. If I should find that I made such a mistake among those invited, I can assure you they would feel my wrath. There is no one I value more than Olivia. The only way to my good side is through her good grace. I hope you ladies enjoy the rest of the evening. Say hello to my wife if you get the chance. I'm sure she would like to meet you."

"Thank you, Duke Chalon. We shall heed your advice." They said before he left them.

"You are a diplomat." Jacob whispered.

"I meant every word." Paul assured him.

About thirty minutes later, we sat to enjoy our meal. Jacob sat among the people Paul wanted him to keep an eye on and Amelia sat next to me.

Paul stood up to address the guests before we ate. "My wife and I would like to thank you all for coming and sharing in the celebration of our marriage. We appreciate your discretion in keeping the world from finding out about Olivia. There are those who still wish to take her away from us. Your continued silence regarding our personal lives will help me to keep her safe. That will not go unnoticed. Now that the food is on the table, let us bless the meal. *Dear Lord Jesus, thank You for Your blessing on this home and my family and guests. May You supply us with Your grace as we face each day. Please bless this meal and those who prepared it. Amen.* Please enjoy your meal. If you wish more, just ask. My staff will be happy to fill your plates again, and we promise not to notice." He sat down and took my hand as they applauded. "How are you holding up tonight?"

"Amelia is such a help to me. I find I really need her by my side." I told him.

Paul looked at Amelia. "Thank you for taking care of my wife."

"You are quite welcome, Duke Chalon. It is a pleasure." She replied.

The meal was enjoyed by everyone. Paul went off with the men after dinner. I invited the ladies to join me in the sitting room. Lady Jacqueline and my mother sat near me to fend off any questions about my past.

"Mama, how long does this continue?" I asked her when I had a chance to pull her away from the crowd.

"Patience, my dear. Ask Amelia to get Jacob's attention. Tell her that you want your husband to know you are growing weary." She said. "Then it is up to him."

I did what she suggested. Amelia left us and arranged for a male servant to pull Jacob from Paul's side to speak with her in the hall. He managed to leave the room unnoticed.

"I knew you would look for me sooner or later." He smiled.

"Jacob, Duchess Olivia is growing weary of the evening. Can you let the Duke know?" She asked.

"Of course." He answered.

"Discreetly." She whispered.

"I know that. Goodnight, Amelia. By the way, you look radiant tonight." He blew her a kiss.

"Stop that and thank you. Now go." She returned to me.

A few minutes later, the men started to collect their wives from the sitting room. I joined my husband and said goodnight to our guests. My mother stayed as our guest. She was given the guest bedroom next to Lady Jacqueline.

Jacob took care of locking up. Then he went into the kitchen and found Amelia there. "You can't seem to stay out of the kitchen." He said.

"I have been in charge of this kitchen for a year. Now it seems so strange living in the mansion part of the house instead of the servants' section. I was just checking to make sure it was clean before I went to bed." She said.

"I'll walk you to your room." He offered.

"We are on the same floor." She reminded him.

"I am very aware of that." He smiled.

"You are a very nice man, Jacob." She said.

"I was hoping to impress you." He replied as he held out his arm as a gesture of escorting her.

She took his arm. "Thank you for getting me out of the kitchen. I like the job I have now. I really like being around the Duchess. She is very nice."

"Yes, she is." He walked her upstairs and to her door. "Goodnight, Amelia."

She opened her door. "Goodnight, Jacob."

Chapter Nine

Sir Douglas entered the house at supper time and met Keith as he was walking down the hall to the dining room. "It is good to see at least one son greeting me as I come in the door."

"Hello, Father." Keith replied. "I could smell the aroma of tonight's meal from my room. I'm looking forward to dinner."

"Give me time to change, and I will join you." His father said.

They sat down a few minutes later to eat together.

"Have you heard from Olivia?" He asked Keith.

"No, but I have heard from Jacob. He found a job as the assistant to some important man in France. He wrote that he loves the job, and he has found a woman he is interested in." Keith told him.

"France? I had no idea his intention was to travel that far." He was surprised and wondered if he should be concerned.

"I was surprised also. I know Jacob understands the language, but I didn't think he could speak it very well. Maybe his desperate attempt to be on his own has motivated him to take risks." Keith said.

"Do you know if he has been in contact with Olivia?" His father asked.

"He did mention seeing her. She is very happy with Paul Stephens and she enjoys being around Paul's family. Father, why won't you consider welcoming them back? I know Charles has mentioned it to you. She is your only daughter." Keith reminded him.

"She betrayed me and embarrassed me in front of the Earl's son. She damaged my reputation almost beyond repair. I look like a fool to them now - a man who cannot control his own daughter. I am in no hurry to welcome her back and certainly my feelings against Paul Stephens are much stronger for taking her to his bed." He replied.

"He married her. She didn't just sleep with him." Keith didn't like the reference his father was making.

"Let's not quarrel about your sister and her husband." His father insisted. "I have good news for you. I wanted to share it with you this evening."

"Tell me." Keith was anxious to hear.

"After years of trying to track down your family and the story of how you came to be on the streets when we found each other, I have a very good answer." His father was very excited to give the news.

"The fact that you seem happy about this must mean something good for me." Keith said. "What did you find out?"

"The men I hired found nothing at all. There was no trail back to your parents and certainly not to your heritage, at least by all the usual courses of investigation. It was actually a woman I ran across who pointed me in the right direction. She said that in some countries royal families put marks on their children, like a family crest, but much smaller. For years I've been looking at that design on your upper arm. I drew it from memory and had someone research it. It is the family mark of the family Chalon. The only reference to that name that I am aware of is the wine that I had contracted to import and market. I have sent a letter to Andre Chalon in France with a drawing of the mark on your arm. I have been waiting for his response."

"You would not have told me all of this to disappoint me with having to wait." Keith said.

"You are right. I received his letter this morning. The first part of the letter is greetings and polite conversation, but the part we are both interested in says, *the design you sent me is indeed the mark that has been used for over one hundred years in my particular family line. The young man you mentioned could not be a cousin as a part of the design would have suggested that. He would have had to be my father's son. I have checked with my family, and we decided to dig up the grave of our dear beloved Collin who disappeared as a small child. My father claimed that Collin had drowned in a lake near our home. He took care to have him buried on our property. When we inspected the coffin, no body was found. The approximate age of the man you mentioned would line up with Collin's age. Be aware that we have not informed our mother of this as she has grieved for Collin's loss for years. It is our belief that our father wanted to give her heart rest as he searched for our brother secretly, and that is why the story of a* discovered body followed by a burial was necessary. Certainly you are invited to meet with me and my brother Philippe in front of the Notre Dame Cathedral in Paris on the ninth day of August at noon. We will direct you and the man you wrote to us about to an expert who will verify that the mark has not been put on his skin to deceive us. If he proves to be our brother Collin, we will welcome you both to join our family and reimburse you for all the expenses this trip will cost you. Certainly a reward for Collin's return will be given to Collin for him to disperse in any manner he wishes."

"That is incredible." Keith said.

"I wish I could go with you for this, but I cannot leave my business. I am sending Charles with you in my place." Sir Douglas told him.

"I don't understand. You should be there. You are the one who took me in and raised me. You sought to find my family. I owe you my very life. You should be there." Keith tried to insist.

"I cannot leave my business; and if disappointment is ahead for you, I don't want to see it. Go with Charles. Have the meeting and write to me about it. Certainly your family is not going to want to part with you again once they discover you are Collin. I am happy to have been part of your life." He said sincerely.

"Father, please reconsider." Keith pleaded.

"No, my son. We will say our goodbyes in a few days. If it works out for you, then enjoy your life. If not, return to me and I will welcome you with open arms." He replied. He couldn't risk stepping onto French soil. He feared charges against him would be waiting for him along with a prison sentence.

"Very well, Father. I will do as you wish. Thank you." Keith finished his meal and left the table to visit Charles.

A few days later they were on their way to Notre Dame Cathedral in Paris. They traveled by boat and then by carriage. They waited in front of the cathedral for fifteen minutes before Andre and Philippe Chalon arrived.

Andre stepped out of the carriage and introduced himself to them.

Charles extended his hand to shake Andre's. "My name is Charles Douglas, and this is my brother Keith. Keith was taken in by my father when he was just a boy. Keith has the mark you seek to identify." Charles told him.

"Is your father on this trip with you?" Andre asked.

"No. He couldn't get away. He is waiting at home in England for news of what you will help us discover here today." Charles told him.

"Please join us in the carriage. I will introduce you to my brother Philippe." Andre directed.

Keith and Charles climbed into the carriage as Andre gave the driver new instructions to return to our home. Then he climbed into the carriage and joined the others. He introduced them to Philippe.

"You understand that we are only being cautious about these circumstances. We would like nothing more than for you to turn out to be our brother. Until we have proof we must keep our enthusiasm in check." Andre explained.

"I understand." Keith responded.

Paul waited in his office once he saw the carriage approaching the mansion. Jacob and I stayed hidden upstairs near the third floor window that looked out over the front of our house. We saw Keith and Charles get out of the carriage.

"Jacob, they look wonderful to me. I am so nervous about this." I told him.

"They will forgive us once they know the whole story. It is Charles I am worried about. I'm not sure he will agree to test Father for the sake of the truth." Jacob said.

"Mr. Charles Douglas, would you please wait in the sitting room while our expert examines the mark on your brother's shoulder? This will take some time. Please be patient with us and make yourself comfortable. I will send a servant to you with some food and drink." Andre told him.

"Thank you." Charles went into the sitting room to wait as Keith followed Andre and Philippe to Paul's office.

"Paul!" Keith was surprised and delighted to see him.

"How are you?" Paul shook his hand.

"Nervous. Are you part of this?" Keith asked.

"Yes, more a part of it than you realize. Take off your shirt." Paul told him as he called in an expert from the hall.

Keith took off his shirt. The man examined the skin and the

mark with a magnifying glass.

"Duke Chalon, it is an original mark made at birth. He is the son of Luc Chalon." He told Paul.

"Duke Chalon?" Keith was stunned.

"Thank you for your service to us. You may leave." Paul told him.

He left and was escorted out the back door so that Charles would not see him.

"Before you overreact, wait for us to explain your life and ours." Paul removed his shirt as did his brothers.

Keith saw the mark on each of them.

"We are your brothers. You were born after me. Philippe and Andre are twins, although they do not look alike. They were born after you. We want you to understand the truth about your disappearance. It will be difficult for you and take some time to explain, but this you will want to hear. We have proof of all of it, even by the hand of your father Sir Douglas." Paul said.

"I'm listening." Keith listened intently as Paul went through the details.

Then Paul handed him the letters to read.

Keith cried. He was devastated. It took him a while to recover enough to speak.

"I am sorry, Keith." Paul felt so bad for him.

Keith wiped his eyes. "This day did not turn out anything like I thought it would."

"Charles is still waiting. Do you think we should explain this to him too?" Paul asked.

"No, certainly not. Even if he did believe it, he would not let me do what I want to about this." Keith told him.

"And what is it you want to do?" Paul asked.

"I want to give my father, Sir Douglas, the chance to redeem himself in my eyes. If he has repented in his heart about his actions and schemes in my life, I will reward him as you promised in your letter. If not, and this has all been for revenge and reward, then I will leave him with nothing. I have a plan to uncover the truth, and I want my family there to witness it." Keith told him.

"Tell us the plan." Paul said.

"Deny my heritage. Tell Charles that the mark was planted as a hoax and failed the test of your expert. I will go home and ask my father to keep looking. His reaction will reveal his heart. When it does, I want witnesses." He said.

"Your father may hurt Olivia if she approaches him." Paul said.

"At a masked ball he won't. He won't know she is there or that you are either." Keith said. "Paul, bring the letters with you."

"How are you going to arrange all this?" Paul asked.

"I don't have to do anything. He has been invited by the

King and Queen of England. He has to go. I will write to him informing him that Charles and I will meet him there. I will promise to give him the news after we arrive. The timing of it is perfect. Since the whole family of Sir Douglas has been invited, I can get you in on my invitation." Keith said. "I am assuming that Olivia and Jacob are here."

"Yes and looking forward to seeing you both." Paul said.

"Not here. Take them to another home and have us meet them there. I don't want Charles to know this is where you all live. I don't want him to see you. Can you arrange that quickly?" Keith asked.

"Yes, of course." Andre said. "I have a cottage house a mile from here. You can meet them there. Paul, use it for your guests if you wish. They need never know it is mine."

Keith smiled. "Get moving Paul. I am about to disappoint my brother. Andre and Philippe, I hope your acting ability is still good."

Paul hugged Keith. "Should we call you Keith or Collin dear brother?"

"Collin is back. Welcome him home, but call me Keith. I am used to that. I may change my mind later." Keith replied.

Andre and Philippe hugged him too.

Paul left and took the back staircase to us. "We are meeting them at another place. We go through the kitchen. Grab some fruit, cheese and bread on the way. We have to feed them something. I will grab the wine."

We ran down the stairs into the kitchen where the staff helped us pack some items quickly. Then Paul ushered us out the back door and into a carriage headed for the cottage.

Keith came out to Charles. Charles stood up waiting for the news.

"I am afraid that the mark your brother has was imposed on him years ago, but is a replica only. It did not pass the test. Our sorrow matches his. We regret you traveled all this way for such disappointing news. We will pay your passage home as we feel that Keith was not trying to deceive us. He was merely a victim." Andre told Charles.

"Thank you." Charles said. "Keith, are you very disappointed?"

"Disappointment does not describe what I feel right now. Let's just go." Keith said.

"Mr. Douglas, I do have good news for both of you. Philippe tells me that the Paul Stephens you mentioned and his wife Olivia are not far from here. My driver can take you to them." Andre offered.

"That would be wonderful." Charles was excited.

"We shouldn't waste the trip." Keith said as Andre escorted them outside to the carriage.

Andre spoke to the driver in French. Then he spoke to Charles and Keith when they were seated. "My driver will wait for you if you need him to. Please let him know."

"Thank you, Andre." Keith said.

"It is my pleasure." Andre smiled. "My brother and I will arrange to have your tickets waiting for you with the harbor master. Leave any time you choose."

"Thank you, Andre. Your family has been very kind." Charles told him.

"Enjoy this time with your family." Andre said as he closed the carriage door.

They pulled away and rode the mile to the cottage. I saw them approaching and wanted to run out to greet them.

"No, Olivia. You cannot see their faces while they travel. You will give us away. I will greet them as they pull up. Wait inside. I will call to you and Jacob. Remember, we are surprised they are here." Paul reminded me.

As the carriage pulled into the front yard Paul went out to greet them. He acted surprised when they stepped out of the carriage. He yelled to me and Jacob, and I rushed at Keith first and hugged him.

"Hello, little sister." He hugged me back. "I've missed you very much."

Then I turned and hugged Charles. "Oh, Charles, I've missed you and Keith so much."

Charles held me close. "You look so grown up all married and all. It was fortunate the Chalon family knew you were here. This is a cute little place for you and Paul. Is this your home?"

Paul interrupted. "No. We are staying here at the gracious

invitation of my brother." He shook hands with Charles and Keith.

"Good thing I was visiting them today, or I would have missed you both." Jacob told them.

"Come inside." Paul invited them.

We sat around and talked about so much. We were laughing and joking with each other. Paul had stories to tell and Jacob told them more about Amelia. Keith asked to take a walk with me alone. We went outside together.

"I understand you are not just the little sister I grew up with." He said.

"Yes, that is true. I am the daughter of a Duchess and I am a Duchess myself. It is a big change for me." I told him.

"How did you handle the information?" He asked.

"Not very well at all. I felt betrayed by my husband for bringing me here. Then I felt betrayed by my father for what he had done to disrupt the life I was supposed to have. Once I found the letters, I grieved for you and for myself. I'm very sorry this has happened to you. Paul told me how upset you were. I completely understand. There are times even now that I cry about us. I wanted to be able to go home at some point and hug the father who raised me. How can I do that now? I love him in spite of this betrayal and that doesn't make sense to my mind. I have found a way to forgive him, but I will never trust him. I am worried about you. If there is no pay off, he might want to carry through with his threat of killing you. Have you considered that?" I asked him.

"Yes, I have. That is why I want witnesses when I tell him. I want him to face all of us at once in a public setting. Then I will leave." He said.

"What about Charles? He will be left to handle this shame alone. Shouldn't we prepare him for it?" I asked him.

"Let me prepare him without telling him the truth. There are suggestions that I can make while we travel back." Keith assured me.

"I will pray for you both." I told him.

"Little sister, you and Jacob are coming with us." Keith informed me.

"It won't be safe for me." I told him.

"Paul would never put you in jeopardy. There is a masked ball, and the whole family has been invited by the King and Queen to attend. Father would not dare to refuse that invitation. I can easily get you, Jacob and Paul in." Keith assured me. "Father will not see you unless you reveal yourself to him. I have not told Charles yet that everyone is going back to join us there. I will let him know when we board the ship."

"When will you leave?" I asked him.

"I'll have Paul take us back to the harbor. Charles and I will travel the way we came and from the information I have, Paul will be taking you and Jacob with him on his ship." Keith told me.

"Keith, are you coming back here to live after you have revealed the truth to Sir Douglas?" I asked him.

"I think I must. I need to get to know my family and discover what I have missed." He said.

"Your mother, Lady Jacqueline, will be overjoyed at your return. She still talks about the child she lost. I can see the love in her eyes for you. I have heard the sorrow of her heart." I told him.

"That is why we must do this quickly. I must know the truth and find out if I have just been a pawn to be used for his own gain, or if he really has loved me as a son." Keith said.

Chapter Ten

We were dressed well for the masked ball. Carriages lined the streets as we traveled to the castle. Charles went in first; then we followed with Keith. We had each marked our masks in the left top corner so that we would be able to keep an eye on each other throughout the ball. Once inside, Paul took me away from Keith. We kept our eyes on him as he pushed through the crowd with Charles to meet Sir Douglas.

A woman approached us. "Good evening." She lowered her mask.

"Mama, how did you get here? I didn't know you were coming." I told her.

"King Henry's ambassador, Lord Theodore, invited me as his guest. Imagine my surprise when I caught a glimpse of my daughter entering the ball. Why didn't you tell me you were coming?" She asked.

"Mama, Sir Douglas is supposed to be here. Keith knows about his kidnapping. He is here to test the heart of Sir Douglas. He wants to tell him in front of us that he is not a Chalon. It is a long story, but we are here to find out the truth of his heart." I explained.

"I would like to witness that discovery myself." She told

me.

"It is your right Mama. Come with us to the balcony. That is where we are to witness this." I told her.

"I will join you there in a moment. I must tell Lord Theodore where I will be." She excused herself and joined us a few minutes later.

We stood together on the balcony where we would not be noticed. We could see that Jacob had already found his spot of observation. A few minutes later, Keith and Charles came out to the balcony with Sir Douglas.

"Tell me the good news, Keith." Sir Douglas removed his mask as Charles and Keith did the same.

"The reward would have served you well, Father, but I did not pass the test. Their expert said that my mark was merely a replica of the Chalon mark. I fear we must keep looking for my heritage or let it go and be content to have each other." Keith said.

"That is absurd. That mark is the mark of the Chalon family. I am sure of it." He was completely frustrated.

"Father, it isn't. It looked like it, but their expert said he was sure. It doesn't matter really. I am your son. That is what matters." Keith tried to comfort him.

"You are not my son! We both know that. You are the son of Duke Luc Chalon. They are robbing you of your birthright and me of my reward. I shall make them pay for this. I did not raise you all these years to be denied now!" He tried to keep his voice down, but he was enraged now.

"What are you saying?" Keith asked him.

"We must go back and make them accept you. First I lose Olivia and my plans for her future, and now you. I will not have it! There is a payoff to my years of sacrifice. They must make up for the loss of my own wife and child. I will have it! I will have it!" He clenched his fists as his face grew more red in color.

Charles looked at Keith. "I can't believe it. You were right about him. Let's go." Charles put his hand on his brother's shoulder.

"Not yet. I owe this to my father Duke Luc Chalon and my mother Jacqueline." Keith told him as Charles removed his hand and stepped back. Keith approached Sir Douglas and stood in front of him. The stance he took surprised Sir Douglas enough to stop him from his ranting. "This day, you have proven your heart to me and to the others who have loved you. I am Collin Chalon, and I have proof that you stole me from my parents and my family just as you stole Olivia from her mother the Duchess Dupree. Yes, there was a reward, but you shall not see a penny of it. Instead, on this night, you will lose your family and the respect we had for you. You are despised in my eyes and heart. I shall ruin you. Make note of that. Your reward shall be your ruin." Keith promised him as we all removed our masks and approached him.

The Duchess Dupree snapped her fingers and guards removed Sir Douglas quietly from the masked ball as we watched. He did not dare to oppose them.

"Mama, what will happen to him now?" I asked her.

"I told King Henry about all of this. Paul provided me with the letters as my evidence. The man who was sent to judge Keith as an heir of Luc and Jacqueline Chalon reported his evidence also. King Henry intervened tonight along with the King and Queen of England. They were aware that we were waiting for a repentant heart. Mercy would have been granted if Sir Douglas had shown one. His title is being removed. All his properties will be inherited by Charles and Jacob. He will be imprisoned for the length of time determined by the King, but his life will be spared. My sorrow goes out to all of you, especially you, Charles Douglas. You have not had the time or the information to grasp hold of the magnitude of your father's sins against us. I pray you will forgive me for being the final step in his downfall. I wish the events had not unfolded in this manner."

"I have not been blind to all of it. I have my own sources of information. I do admit this last bit with Keith was a surprise. I believed Keith had failed the test, but I did know about Olivia. I had her followed after she married Paul. I wanted to make sure she was safe and protected. I received monthly reports on her. You see, I am her big brother and I love her. It was my duty to uncover the truth and make sure she was safe. I knew she was in the Chalon mansion, but I did not know that Paul was Duke Chalon. My contact never included that in his report. I thought she was visiting his relatives. Keith fed me stories about the possibilities if he had been found to be Collin Chalon. I thought it was just his talent at telling amusing tales. To his credit he did prepare me for some of this. I do appreciate your apology Duchess Dupree. On behalf of my family, I do apologize to you for the loss my father caused your family." Charles said.

"I realize this is a unique time when sorrow and anger could fill our lives, but let us make a choice tonight to celebrate each other. We have overcome so much, and we are destined to overcome more. Let's join the masked ball. No one here except a chosen few know what happened tonight. Father was removed discreetly. I choose to enjoy the ball, and I hope my brothers and sister will join me. Sorrow can wait another day." Jacob said.

"He is right. After the ball, come to my house. I have plenty of room for all of you to stay comfortably. We can visit with each other for as long as all of you want to stay." Charles had shaken off the shock and put on a smiling face.

"Sounds like a good plan. Come, Olivia, let's enjoy the celebration." Paul took my hand, and we left the balcony with the others.

It was a glorious night of dancing and fun. We were honored to be included in the invitation of the King and Queen. Mama returned to Lord Theodore. Charles, Keith and Jacob danced with the single ladies who had been invited. Jacob stayed near the ones who were a tinge ugly. He didn't want to return to Amelia and have to confess that he danced with beautiful women. The ladies adored his attention, and they had very nice personalities so he wasn't suffering much.

At the end of the evening I kissed Mama goodbye and told her that I wasn't sure how long we would be staying in England.

She hugged me. "Olivia, don't rush life. It goes by too fast. If you enjoy being here with Paul, then stay as long as you like. I will visit when you return to France."

"Mama, do not tell Lady Jacqueline about Keith. Let her four sons do it."

"I will not say a word. I promise." She smiled. "God bless you all."

The rest of them said goodnight to her before we left the ball together. We decided that all of us would sleep at Charles' house that night so that we could stay up together and talk more. After breakfast, we went to the house I had known so well with my brothers. It seemed strange walking in and being aware of our current circumstances.

"Jacob, you are welcome to keep this house. None of us need it and there is no debt required for you to pay." Keith told him.

"I have no objections to that." Charles said.

"We don't have to make any firm decisions now." Jacob said. "I am in love with Amelia. If she agrees to come back here to live, I will keep the house and help Charles with the business. If she wants to stay in France, then we can sell the house and split the money."

"You and Charles split the money. Olivia and I have an inheritance and a destiny." Keith said.

"I agree." I told them.

"One thing I will tell you. If all of you decide to live in France, then I am selling the business and joining you there. I have no one to love here. Maybe I'll have better luck in France." Charles said.

Jacob looked around. "That is entirely a better idea. We need a fresh start Charles. Let's sell it all and join them. I already have my eye on a few women who will impress you. They are beautiful, smart, and single. Let's clean out this place, keep what we want or need, and sell the rest. We can put some money in trust for Father. As despicable as he has been, should he get out, he'll need some cash."

"That sounds like a very good idea." Charles smiled. "Let's start sorting out the things for the auctioneer."

The next month we sold the house, the items in the house, the business and Charles' house. The money was substantial for Charles and Jacob.

Before we left we took the time to visit my Aunt Lucille and my Uncle Peter. They were very happy to welcome us into their home.

"Olivia, darling, I am quite amazed at the story of your life. Your uncle and I had no idea that any of this had happened. We love all of you so completely. You have to know that you have been like a daughter to us. The boys, I mean these young men, are so much in our hearts." Aunt Lucille hugged each of us.

"We wanted to say our goodbyes to you and Uncle Peter. Thank you for your support all these years. You have truly blessed each of us." Charles said to my aunt as he hugged her.

"You take good care of yourselves. Write to us often. We will miss all of you." Uncle Peter told us.

It was a tearful goodbye. We made our way from their

home to Paul's ship. The voyage was difficult emotionally for my brothers and me. The final farewell to the people we loved pulled at our hearts. After we got off the ship we got into a carriage together and headed for Chalon mansion.

"How soon will you introduce me to my mother?" Keith asked Paul as he stepped out of the carriage.

"Give me a moment to arrange it." Paul said. He spoke with a few of the servants who were there to take in the luggage. They ran off in different directions. Then he returned to Keith. "Our brothers will meet us here in an hour. Mother is due back from her shopping just after that. I have the servants preparing smelling salts. I will be surprised if she does not faint. Andre and Philippe will join us in the sitting room to tell her. Be prepared for fainting and tears. Of all of us, you look most like our father. He would have loved that. He was jealous that the rest of us have more of our mother's features to our faces."

"Come with me, brothers. I will show you your rooms and give you a tour of the mansion while we wait for Andre and Philippe." I told them as I stepped out of the carriage.

Amelia saw Jacob entering the house first and alone. She ran into Jacob's arms and kissed him. "I missed you. I was so afraid you would not come back to me."

Keith and Charles were a little jealous of their brother as they stepped through the doorway with Paul and me.

"We can never get good help around here any more." Paul sounded serious.

I wanted to hit him.

Amelia heard him and realized what had happened. She took him seriously. She broke off her hug with Jacob. "Duke Chalon, I am so sorry for my bad manners. Please forgive me." She apologized.

Paul laughed. "Just this once I will make allowances. Next time drag him away before you kiss him. Go back to what you were doing, but do it in private."

"Thank you, Duke Chalon." Amelia grabbed Jacob by the hand and dragged him into the sitting room and shut the door. She jumped into his arms again and kissed him several times repeatedly. "I have really missed you."

"Amelia, this is a surprise to me. You barely gave me the time of day when I left." He pulled her away from his lips.

"I wanted you to want me more. I thought you liked the chase. When you did not return, day after day I worried that you wouldn't and that I had lost you." She explained.

"You haven't lost me at all. I love this greeting. I love you." He kissed her, and she was more enthusiastic than ever.

After a few minutes, he took a breath. "Amelia, you have to marry me. I can't let a girl like you get away from me."

She kissed his neck.

"Stop please. I'm just a man, and we are in the sitting room of Duke Chalon. I can't believe I am saying this."

"You are English. French girls are too much for you, yes?"

He laughed and then she laughed.

"Listen here, little Miss French girl, you are going to marry me very quickly because I like this greeting too much to remain single." He said.

"Are you asking me or telling me?" She whispered as she nibbled on his ear.

"Amelia Francine DeGarmo, will you marry me?" He asked.

She kissed his lips again and whispered yes.

"Don't I have to ask your father or something?" He asked when she gave him a chance.

"No, my sweet morsel." She ran her fingers gently across his lips.

"Stop this. Why not? Don't you have a father?" He asked.

"I do, but he would kill you first. He hates the English." She answered.

"You have to be joking." He said.

"I wish I were. He is a small person, a dwarf. He is away in the circus. My mother is with him. She has a lot of facial hair. Fortunately for you, I do not resemble her side of the family." She kissed him on the neck again.

He was laughing. "Be serious." He turned her around so that she couldn't kiss him any more and restrained her with his arms. "You are driving me crazy."

"Oh, so you think this will stop my pursuit of you?" She

whispered.

"Amelia! Stop now." He was cracking up laughing. "What about your father, the truth?"

"I told him that I love you, and I was waiting for you to ask me to marry you. He is waiting to meet you." She told him.

"Now can I let go of you and have you stop kissing me?" He asked.

"Yes. I have work to do. You can meet my father tomorrow evening. I will arrange it. Dress nicely. Make sure to impress him." She replied as he let her go.

"You are too much." He smiled at her.

"I know. That is why you love me." She kissed him on the cheek and left him in the sitting room alone.

Jacob sat down for a few minutes before Charles walked into the room.

"Words cannot express how jealous I am about that greeting you got at the door." Charles said to him.

"I am still recovering from the greeting I got behind closed doors." Jacob told him.

"Better or worse?" Charles asked.

"Beyond better. I absolutely love her. I asked her to marry me, and she said yes. Now I have to meet her father tomorrow and ask him." Jacob explained.

"Good thing we skipped the tour that included this room.

Does she have a sister?" Charles asked.

"No, but she has a beautiful cousin, Gabriella. I will make sure to introduce you." Jacob said as he got up from the couch. "I'd better go unpack. If you are hungry, just go into the kitchen and ask them to make you something. You speak French. You shouldn't have a problem with the translation."

Nearly an hour later, Andre and Philippe arrived. They waited together with Keith and Paul for Lady Jacqueline. She came in smiling and cheery after her time shopping. Paul greeted her at the door. He took her packages and handed them to a servant.

"Come, Mother. My brothers and I want you to meet someone." He took her hand and brought her into the sitting room.

Keith stood up as she entered. "Good day, Lady Jacqueline."

She looked at her sons. "Doesn't anyone have the good manners to introduce this young man?"

"These are unusual circumstances, Mother. We have to hold off our introduction until you are aware of the unique story about his life." Andre told her.

"Very well. I shall sit down and listen. Please have a seat, Sir, while this mystery is being revealed to me." She sat down across from him.

"Mother, this man has information about our brother Collin. The story is long but necessary." Paul told her.

"Collin? Really? Please begin." She asked Keith.

"When I was a child, I was told by the man who took me in that he had rescued me from the streets. He declared I was an orphan and named me Keith. I grew up in his home with three of his natural born children. At least I thought so at the time. A short time ago, I learned that my sister in this house was really the kidnapped daughter of Duchess Dupree. You know her as Olivia, the girl who married your son. I was raised as her older brother Keith. After Olivia's marriage to Paul, my father, Sir Douglas, began to treat me with an overly generous spirit of favor. He showered wealth in my direction while all the time shunning his youngest son Jacob. I was delighted with the attention but suspicious as to why he would treat me this way. Within a short time, he revealed to me that he was searching for my parents and had been since the day he found me. One evening, he claimed that he had found the missing link, a mark on my upper arm. He claimed that he had researched the mark and that it was like the crest of a family but smaller and that it belonged to this family. I made the trip here to discover if I was indeed a member of your family, Lady Jacqueline."

"Is this some kind of cruel joke? I have no other sons than these, and Collin was buried years ago after his tragic death." She was upset. "My husband was faithful. He would not have another son."

"Mother, Olivia discovered letters that Father had secretly hidden away in his desk. I have them if you would like to read them, but in essence they say that Sir Douglas planned revenge against our father and the Duchess Dupree for the deaths of his wife and child. They also imply that not only did Sir Douglas kidnap Olivia from the Duchess, but he also kidnapped Collin.

In the letter to Father, he threatened to kill Collin should Father ever attempt to pull the two of them out of his hand. I dug up the grave and looked in the coffin myself. It is empty. Collin was never discovered. Father only told you that so that your heart could rest. He worked for years trying to find a way to get Collin back, but each time Sir Douglas had moved or the attempt would have jeopardized his life. Father's hands were tied. He couldn't get him back." Paul explained.

"I don't believe you. This story has been conspired to torment me." She objected.

"No, Mother. All of us have verified the letters and the grave. All of us have seen the mark on Keith's arm. He is our brother Collin. He is your son." Philippe knew he had convinced her.

Keith didn't know what to do as he watched tears fall from her eyes. She covered her mouth with her hand as she looked at him.

"Mother, look at him. He has Father's features: the eyes, the strong chin, the dark hair. He stands like Father and the tone of his voice is very similar. No one can deny that he is Collin." Andre said.

She held out her arms to Keith as she cried and he came to her and knelt down in front of her. She held on to him and wept as he held on to her.

"I'm sorry for causing you pain." Keith apologized as they held on to each other.

She couldn't speak; she just cried. It took quite a while for her to start to relax. She let go of him and wiped her tears. "This is an awful homecoming for you." Her voice strained with emotion as she looked into the face of the son she believed was lost to her. "I have missed you every day that you have been gone. I have searched my heart trying to find the reason for your death and how we could have prevented it. Now you kneel in front of me a grown man. You do look like Luc. You have his eyes and his strength. You have grown into such a handsome young man. Come, come, sit beside me." She invited him.

He got up and sat on the couch next to her and held her hands. "I know you want to call me Collin. Sir Douglas named me Keith. After all that he has done to this family I would like to leave that name behind, but I cannot do that just yet. I am so used to being Keith. We all need time to absorb what has happened to us. Call me Collin if you wish. I will not be offended, but I might not answer to it as quickly as you like right now."

"Keith suits you. It is a strong name for a strong person. Sir Douglas gave you the name God gave him to give you. The Collin I was familiar with is not sitting next to me; he has transformed into the man God would have him be. You are a new man with a new name. I will have all your documents changed, and you will be known to us as Keith Collin Chalon, if you agree."

"You are a very wise woman. No wonder my father loved you so much." Keith told her.

"Your fortune will be restored to you." Paul said. "My brothers and I have agreed to it. You will not have to fight for your place in this family. We are overjoyed to be able to offer it back to you."

"I would like to spend time with each of you so that you get to know me and I get to know you better. I would like to hear the stories of your youth. Mother, I would like you to tell me as much about my father as you can. I want to know him through your eyes and heart." Keith told her.

"I promise to do that as soon as you get to know me better." She said. "I am jealous of our time together. I won't give you up easily."

"Mother, this day we share Keith alone. Tomorrow we share him with our wives and children. We have arranged for a family gathering to overwhelm him with nieces and nephews and our chatty wives." Andre told her.

"Are you up to that my son?" She smiled at him.

"With you by my side, I am up to anything." He assured her.

"You are your father's son." She patted his hand.

"Brothers, can you leave me alone with our mother for a few minutes?" He asked them.

They left the room and closed the door.

"Please stand up, Mother." He asked her.

She did.

"I don't remember your love. For years I lacked it. I am looking forward to it. Our first hug was full of tears. I would like one full of love. Will you hug me again and hold on as long as you possibly can?" He requested.

"I cannot promise not to cry." She said as tears filled her eyes again.

"I cannot promise that either." He wrapped his arms around her as she did the same.

They held each other for a very long time in silence, love and tears. When they came out of the sitting room they could smell the aroma of tasty food coming from the kitchen.

"I know I am hungry." Keith told her.

"Do you want to snack before dinner?" She asked.

"Yes." He answered.

She spotted Amelia coming down the hall. "Amelia, take Keith into the kitchen and find him something to snack on before dinner." She said in French.

"Yes, Lady Jacqueline." Amelia responded in English. "Come this way, Keith."

"Go. I must freshen up before we eat together." She said.

Keith walked to the kitchen with Amelia. "You are the girl who met my brother Jacob at the door."

"Yes, I am." She said proudly.

"You don't lack confidence, do you?" Keith observed.

"You are like him. You have that subtle wit that makes me laugh." She said.

"He's a sweet kid." Keith remarked.

"You are wrong. Jacob is a very sweet man, and I love him very much. Your teasing ways will not work on me." She warned him.

"Jacob warned you about me, didn't he?" Keith asked as they reached the kitchen.

"Yes, he did. Now let's find you something to eat." She went through the kitchen holding up items like fruit and bread to him.

He smiled and shook his head no.

Then she got to the cookies and pastries and found his weakness. She went to hand feed him a cookie and he grabbed her hand.

"Amelia, where I come from your actions would be considered flirting with me. Don't test the waters between Jacob and me. I am loyal to my brother and this kind of action will cause us a problem. Don't do it again for any reason."

She smiled. "Now, I can respect you."

"Amelia, have you been made aware of my position here?" He asked her.

"No. Did Lady Jacqueline give you a job?" I asked him.

"No, Amelia. I am her son." He told her.

"How can that be? You are Jacob's brother. Is this the way the English come into a family?" She asked.

"It is a little more complicated than that. I'm sure Jacob will explain the details to you. I have no wish to go over them right now. My name is Keith Collin Chalon. I am the son of Luc and Jacqueline Chalon and the brother to Duke Paul Chalon." He said.

"Oh my." She looked worried. "My apologies for my forward behavior toward you. Please forgive me, Lord Chalon."

"Amelia, I did not mean to upset you. I am just getting used to this myself. I realize you viewed me as just Jacob's brother. As soon as my birthright is explained, the rest of the staff will be aware of the way we treat each other. I was just giving you a word to the wise." He explained.

"I understand, Lord Chalon." She said.

"Is it possible that you could continue to call me Keith or is that against the rules here?" He asked her.

"I could whisper your name. For the sake of protocol, I must address you as Lord Chalon in public. If there is a possibility of being overheard, I cannot risk punishment." She told him.

"Thank you for explaining that. In private, whisper Keith. I like that better coming from my future sister-in-law. You should go. I am fine here eating these cookies." He told her.

"Yes, Keith." She whispered.

Chapter Eleven

"Olivia, I feel like we haven't relaxed in days. How do you feel about spending the morning in my arms under the blankets?" He asked me as I was just starting to wake up.

"Is that your idea of relaxing?" I smiled at him.

"Maybe relaxing isn't the right word." He admitted as he wrapped me up in his arms and kissed me.

"You are required to whisper to me the goals and secret details of our future life together while we indulge in this kind of relaxation." I told him.

He whispered in my ear. "We shall have at least three children." Then he kissed me on the neck.

"Keep talking. I love these romantic conversations." I encouraged him.

He took a moment to look into my eyes and smile at me. "You are completely captivating to me. I love you, Olivia. You are the most cooperative wife I've ever had."

"You shall have to pay for the second half of that statement, Paul Chalon." I laughed.

It was a good thing the entire third floor was ours alone.

Our laughter and joy would have awakened the soundest of sleepers.

About lunch time, our guests started to arrive to meet Keith.

"Get dressed, you lovely thing. We have guests." He jumped out of bed when he heard them exiting their carriages and coming to the front door.

"They will know I have spent my time with you alone." I told him as I rushed to find something to wear.

"They will know nothing." He assured me. "Even if they suspected our attention to each other, this is France. People are expected to be romantic here."

He finished dressing before me and went downstairs to welcome our guests.

"We wondered where you were all morning." His mother remarked.

He smiled and ignored her remark. He went on to greet his brother Andre and Andre's wife Marcella. He hugged his little nephews, Jon and Luc. "Go out to the back. The staff has set up tables for us near the garden and toys for the children." He turned and greeted Philippe and his wife Camille. Then he picked up his two nieces, Lauren who was nearly four and Jazel who just turned two years old the week before. "You are both beautiful like your mother." He told them.

"Where is Olivia?" Camille asked.

"Perfection takes time." He replied.

"Where is this brother Philippe has told me about?" Camille asked.

Paul looked to Jacob for an answer.

"He is already waiting outside." Jacob told him.

Everyone headed outside to share their time with Keith. When I came outside to join them, little Lauren was making her way toward Keith.

"Uncle Keith." She said in French.

He didn't understand.

Amelia came to his rescue. "Lord Chalon, she called you Uncle Keith."

"I have no idea how to respond. Will you speak for me?" He asked her.

"Yes, of course. What would you like to say to her?"

"Tell her I am delighted to be her Uncle Keith." He said.

Amelia told the little girl.

Then Lauren held out her arms and spoke to him. Amelia translated the request and Keith picked her up. They shared a wonderful conversation with each other via Amelia.

"I shall ask my Mama to teach me English." She told him.

Amelia translated.

"I shall ask my Mama to teach me French." He replied.

When Amelia translated, Lauren laughed and then she

kissed him on the cheek.

He was delighted with the affection from his niece and kissed her cheek before her put her down. "She is very smart."

"You have won her over, Lord Chalon." Amelia said.

"Amelia, we have to find away around all this formality." Keith told her. "I find I am frustrated with it. Do you have any suggestions?"

"It is Duke Chalon's house." She hinted.

Keith walked right over to Paul. "Can we talk for a minute?"

"Yes." Paul went away from the others with him. "What is it?"

"This Lord and Duke stuff is simply annoying. Here my brother Jacob's fiancée is translating for me; and at every statement where she could just refer to me as Keith, she calls me Lord. I hate it. Can you make a rule of some kind that she can drop the formalities around me?" Keith asked.

"Is this just with her? Your title is Lord now. Jacob will be calling you Lord and so will Charles, even Olivia at times." Paul explained.

"You can't be serious." Keith said.

"Yes, I am serious. Maybe Mother should give you lessons about royal requirements." Paul suggested.

"I will seek her advice on those matters very soon. Is it possible now to let my entire family just call me Keith, including Amelia?" He asked.

"As long as no one outside the family is present and only among our staff of servants. Will that satisfy you?" Paul asked.

"Yes. It would be a delight to my ears." He said.

Paul got everyone's attention. He announced Keith's request in French and then in English. Then he announced his solution in French and then in English. Everyone applauded the decision.

We had a wonderful day together. Keith enjoyed everyone's company. At the end of the day he sat outside under the stars with Charles.

"Charles, I want a family." Keith told him.

"I completely agree, Keith. I want that too." Charles said.

"We should get Jacob right on that." They both said at once and then laughed.

"He seems to be doing well for himself." Charles pointed to his brother spending time with Amelia under the moonlight.

"She's very interesting." Keith remarked.

"And beautiful." Charles mentioned.

"Jacob is visiting her father tomorrow afternoon. She told him her father hates the English and would kill him. Then she told him that her father was a dwarf in the circus. She keeps him laughing." Keith said.

"You need that in a marriage. There has to be laughter. I don't want a dull woman who takes everything so seriously. It will kill my spirit if I have to deal with a nag who complains constantly. I don't really care if she is stunning. A plain girl with wisdom and a sense of humor along with a willingness to love me would be ideal." Charles said.

"You are so practical Charles." Keith remarked.

"And you are a romantic. You should settle that in your heart before you choose your one true love, or romance will pull you away from her. The grass is not greener when you look for it on the back of someone you promised to love. Love is a choice sometimes. It has to endure to grow strong. Remember that, especially now that you have been elevated to a higher position in life." Charles told him.

"You're right. I've bounced around from one woman to the next. I don't think it is the romance because they are all similar in that respect. I think it is because I find something I like in one and then something else I find in another. If I could just find that woman who has all the qualities I look for, I am sure I would be satisfied." He said.

"Work on those qualities with her. You could ask God to change you a little too. Not all your ways are good ways. You're not perfect." Charles reminded him.

"I'm as close as the right woman will get to perfection." He joked.

"Sure, you and I both. That is why we are out here under the stars talking to each other instead of having a beautiful woman in our arms like our brother over there. This is frustrating. I'm going inside. They look like they will need some privacy soon." Charles got up from his chair.

"You're right." Keith got up and followed him inside.

Jacob looked over as he saw his brothers leave. "Finally, I thought they would be watching us all night."

"Is that why you were limiting my affection?" Amelia asked.

"Amelia, you know that is not the reason." He replied.

"I know. You want to feel honorable when you speak with my father. He doesn't speak English. I will have to translate for you." She said.

"No, you won't. I know enough French now to ask him for his blessing." Jacob insisted.

"He is deaf in both ears." She said.

"Will you stop? I don't care if he is a blind, deaf, dwarf holding a gun on me while he kisses your hairy mother. I am going to ask for his blessing on our marriage." Jacob insisted.

"He walks with a limp and drool falls from his mouth when he speaks. Don't let those things distract you." She said.

He cracked up laughing and then he kissed her. "I can't stand not being married to you. I want you now and you know it."

"Oh, my sweet morsel." She kissed his lips. "Keep thinking honorable thoughts as you remember my kisses on your lips."

"You are not helping me. Let's go." He stopped holding her close and took her hand. "I am walking you inside and up to your room. You will lock your door. Then I will go into my room and lock my door. Tomorrow I meet your father, and he has to be convinced that I love you and that I am an honorable man."

"Disregard his missing teeth. He lost them fighting with the last man who asked to marry me." She told him.

Jacob kept laughing.

"My mother speaks for him now. You can ask him the questions, but look at her for the answers. Try not to stare at the mole on the end of her nose or the long black hair that hangs from her chin. She is sensitive about her appearance when she is not under the big tent." She tried to be serious but the sound of Jacob's laughter was contagious and caused her to laugh.

"Go inside, you crazy person." He told her as he continued to laugh.

"Goodnight, my sweet morsel." She whispered to him.

"Goodnight, Amelia." He watched her shut her door and laughed all the way to his room.

The next day, Jacob took Amelia with him in a carriage to meet her father. The section where he lived was not the poorest section, but close to it. Amelia held his hand as they approached the door. She knocked twice and opened the door. "Mama. Papa." She called out as they entered.

Her mother spoke French and invited them to sit at the table. Her father looked like a very strong man. He stood up, shook Jacob's hand and motioned for him to sit down at the table with his wife and Amelia.

Amelia introduced Jacob and explained to her father what he did for a living and how he had helped her to get out of the kitchen.

Her father was thrilled that she was the assistant to the Duchess.

Jacob asked for Amelia's hand in marriage and Mr. DeGarmo's blessing. He was happy to give it. Her mother wanted to know when the wedding would take place. Jacob told her as soon as possible. He didn't want them to wait.

"Do you have a home for my daughter?" Her father asked.

"No, Sir. We live in the mansion." Jacob answered.

"That is not good." Her father said. "A husband and a wife need privacy to work out the good and the bad. The Duke will not want you to fight with your wife in his mansion. He will not want you to make up with your wife either in his mansion."

"You may be right about that. I promise that before we get married I will have a home for us." Jacob told him.

"You are a good man. You know how to listen." Her father said.

"Thank you. I will let you know the date of the wedding so you can be there." Jacob said.

"No. It is enough that we know our daughter is marrying a fine young man. Your people are wealthy and particular about who is around them. We are poor, but happy. We understand that we will draw attention away from our daughter as she marries you. It should be her day alone. She knows that we love her." Mr. DeGarmo said.

"A father should give the bride to the groom." Jacob wanted him there.

"Stand up, Jacob." He said.

Jacob stood up next to Amelia. Her father kissed her cheek. "I give you to this man as his bride. You have made me proud all the days of my life, little one. Go make a good life with Jacob Douglas. Have many healthy babies and bring them by occasionally to visit us. God bless you both." He took Amelia's hand and put it into Jacob's. "I give the treasure of my heart to you, Jacob Douglas. Take good care of her."

"I will." Jacob was impressed with Amelia's father and his love for her.

Her mother got up and kissed them both on the cheek. "God will bless this marriage. My prayers have been answered. Go now both of you. This is no place for you. I love you."

Amelia kissed her mother and father goodbye on the cheek. "Thank you." She whispered to each of them. Then she left with Jacob, and they returned to the mansion. Jacob spoke with Paul about marrying Amelia and finding a home for them that would allow them the privacy they needed.

"As my wedding present to you both, I will have a cottage built for you on the estate. We can draw up the plans together. You will have your privacy and be close enough that I may reach you in an emergency. It is important to Olivia that Amelia be close by." Paul told him.

"That is an extraordinary gift and very much appreciated. I

do not mean to step out of line, but how long will that take? I am anxious to marry Amelia." Jacob was careful to use the right tone when asking.

Paul smiled. "We will draw up your specifications tonight and I will hire the people necessary to start on the project and stay with it until it is done. I cannot tell you at this moment how long it will take. I can promise you it will be built well and as quickly as possible."

"Thank you very much, Duke Chalon." Jacob said.

"Jacob, even now you stumble with our familiarity. It must be in your family line. When we are alone, call me Paul. You are not only considered my brother, but you are the closest friend I have here. It is Duke Chalon when others are present and only to set the example of respect and consideration of my title." Paul told him.

"I shall remember that." Jacob said.

"Now, let's get on with the work of the day. I have a few assignments for you." Paul told him.

I interrupted the meeting by walking into Paul's office. "Darling, do you know where Charles and Keith have gone? I've looked everywhere in the mansion, but they are not here."

"Andre has taken them to find property. Each of your brothers desires an estate of his own. I suspect they will be gone all day." Paul replied.

"Good morning, Jacob." I said cheerfully.

"Good morning." He smiled at me.

"Is that all?" Paul seemed impatient with me to leave.

I recognized the attitude. My father Sir Douglas used it when I disturbed him. He hurt my feelings with his impatience to have me leave. "Yes. Forgive me for disturbing you."

"Is something wrong?" Jacob asked.

"I am annoyed with trivial questions." He said.

"Not that I want to get involved, but the question was important to Olivia. She came to the one man in this place who has all the answers, the one she trusts. Your attitude will put you at a disadvantage." Jacob said.

"How is that?" Paul asked.

"Olivia will either go to someone else and you will miss her smile when you solve her problem, or she will not share her trivial concerns with you. When the wall goes up it will be harder to take down." Jacob advised him.

"I will make a note of it." Paul went on to the assignments of the day.

Keith and Charles returned that afternoon. Charles was satisfied he had found a place to live. He had arranged to purchase a manor ten miles from us. It was large enough to live comfortably and have visiting guests. He was looking forward to starting a family and hiring a staff and workers for the land. Keith hadn't found anything he liked yet. He agreed to help Charles set up his estate and live with him until he could find something of his own.

Chapter Twelve

The cottage was nearly complete, and I knew arrangements for Jacob's wedding needed to start. I spoke with my husband before we went to bed. "Paul, I would like to have Jacob marry Amelia here. We could arrange a small gathering of people to celebrate their wedding with us. It doesn't have to be anything too big. Would that be alright with you?" I asked him.

"Of course. Make the plans and get the staff to help you. Keep those of nobility who would look down on them out of your plans. You know who they are." He said.

"Thank you. I haven't mentioned it to them yet. I wanted to talk to you first." I told him as I brushed my hair out in front of the mirror.

"We have such an odd family. Brothers who are not brothers and brothers who are brothers but were not brothers. I think it confuses some of the people who visit us. When I married you, I married complications." He said as he came to me. He pushed my hair out of the way of the back of my neck and kissed me there. "How long will this take?"

I smiled and he could see my reflection in the mirror. I handed him the brush. "Help me and it will take less time."

He took the brush and started brushing out my long hair

gently. "I am a Duke. I run a vineyard and make lots of money and now I am reduced to brushing out my wife's hair once again."

I laughed. "You like to do this. You told me so."

"It is only because it is a beautiful part of who you are." He said.

"It is because you melt my heart when you do things like this and you know the reward comes later." He saw me smile at him in the mirror.

"Olivia, you used to come to my office more during the day. Why have you stopped doing that?" He asked as he continued to brush my hair.

"I don't want to get in your way." I told him.

"You are not in my way." He said.

"For years, Sir Douglas worked in his office when he was home. When I was a girl I used to want to visit him in his office. He would give me the same look you have given me lately, like I am annoying you with my presence. I know the look Paul and the attitude. I know I am not mistaken." I told him.

"You're right. I have been impatient with you. I've had my mind on other things that I thought were more important than your visits and questions for me. I was wrong to treat you that way. Please visit me again. Ask me any question you wish. If I am busy, I will get up and affectionately walk you to the door. I will make sure to kiss you before you leave me." He promised.

"You want a baby." I accused him of having a motive

behind this change of heart.

"Of course I do." He put the brush down, and I stood up in front of him.

"I am just eighteen Paul. We haven't been married very long at all. I like us together the way we are now. I'm not ready to have a baby just yet. I love giving you undivided attention." I told him.

"Are you preventing us from having a baby somehow?" He asked me.

"Not that I know of, but I am not saddened that it hasn't happened yet. I think we are blessed to have this time together without a child. Can't we just enjoy it without having you wonder about what might be wrong with me?" I asked him.

"Olivia, just let the doctor examine you. That is all I am asking." He said.

"No. Absolutely not. Stop asking me to do that. I know your mother started this. Since she mentioned it to you I have been tormented by your continual persistence to have me checked out by a doctor. A baby will come when a baby wants to come." I walked away from him and climbed under the covers. I was upset with being pressured once again.

He climbed into the bed next to me and touched me on the shoulder. "You are upset with me."

"Go to sleep, Paul." I was on my side holding on to my pillow.

"Olivia, please don't be like this." He leaned over and kissed me on the cheek.

I rolled over to face him. "How can you expect me to love you when you are convinced I am inadequate?"

"I never said that." He denied it.

"When we were first together, all you wanted was me and all I wanted was you. Now each time, it seems you are in it to make a baby. All I hear about is your disappointment about my not being pregnant. I think that has consumed you. That is why you were annoyed with my intrusion into your office. You look at me and you see someone who is broken and needs to be fixed. I don't reach the expectations you had of me. I don't want to love a man who will find disappointment in me. Just go to sleep." I rolled over and hid from him in my pillow.

"Olivia, that is ridiculous. Stop hiding in that pillow." He pulled it out from under me and made me face him. "I'm not disappointed in this part of our marriage. I look forward to holding you in my arms and loving you. I want you every day and it has nothing to do with making a baby. I don't think about making a baby when we are together. I think about it at random times during the day but not every day. You have never been a disappointment to me. You are amazing and wonderful. I love you. Would you deny your husband the touch of your lips or the fulfillment of this time together? I promise you, it is just you and me together. I think only about how wonderful you are and how much I love you. Nothing else enters my heart when I am with you. Please don't turn away from me."

"You mean it? I am not a disappointment?" I asked.

"I meant every word. Olivia, please share your love with me." He kissed me once and again. "No one is more important to me than you."

I couldn't resist his gentle ways and loving words.

The next morning, I told Jacob and Amelia that we would be having the wedding ceremony outside behind the mansion. I asked them for a list of the people they wanted to invite. Both of them were excited about the idea. Jacob insisted that we invite her parents, and I agreed. Amelia was reluctant to go along with our idea.

"They won't be comfortable among people who have so much elegance and standing in life. They don't even have anything good enough to wear among all of you." She said.

"Nonsense. I can provide your parents with suitable garments. They should see their daughter get married and be involved in our wedding day." Jacob said.

"Jacob, you assume too much." Amelia was upset with him and walked away from the plans.

"Excuse me, Olivia. I think I need to find out why she is so upset." Jacob left me and followed Amelia until he caught up with her. "Amelia, talk to me. Don't just walk away."

She turned around and started yelling at him in French. Her hands were waving around as she carried on. She spoke so fast he didn't catch all of it, but he did understand the last part.

"Did you just call me an idiot?" He was surprised. "Amelia, speak English. The way you ramble on, I can only understand part of what you are saying."

She seemed more frustrated with having to repeat it in English. She took his hand and brought him to the table near the garden. He sat down across from her.

"Explain why you are so upset. I don't understand." He said.

"My father already told you that he did not want to come to the wedding. He gave you his reasons. He blessed our marriage, and he was very kind about the whole thing. Why do you insist on having him here? He doesn't want to be here, and I don't want him here. You never asked me what I wanted. You just assumed for me. Now I will look like the bad daughter because I don't want my parents at my wedding." She explained.

"Is it because they are poor?" Jacob asked.

"Jacob, I don't want them here. Can't you just let me have the wedding the way I want it?" She was still upset with him.

"Yes, of course. Amelia, I get the feeling you are hiding something from me. Are you hiding something about your family from me? If you are, please tell me what it is."

"You are not marrying my family. You are marrying me. My family has nothing to do with us." She answered.

"So you are hiding something? What is it? If you can't trust me with the information, then why are we getting married?" He asked her.

"I don't know. Why are we getting married?" She ran from him crying.

Paul came out of the mansion and saw Amelia run from Jacob. "What happened?" He asked Jacob.

"I have no idea. I wanted to invite her parents to the wedding and she screamed at me about it. She is hiding something about her parents, but she won't tell me what it is. What could be so bad that she couldn't tell me?"

"Go to her Jacob. If you love her, don't let her alone until she tells you." Paul advised him.

"She will lock me out of her room." Jacob said.

"You're engaged. The key to her room is in the top drawer of my desk. The keys are marked. Put it back at the end of the day and don't pick it up again without my permission." Paul told him.

"Thank you." Jacob ran to the desk and grabbed the key. Then he headed up the staircase to Amelia's room. "Amelia, open the door and talk to me please."

"Go away. The wedding is cancelled." She yelled back.

He unlocked the door, stepped into the room and locked the door again. "I am not leaving this room until you tell me what is going on. I love you, and you are not cancelling our wedding. Whatever it is that you have been hiding, I insist you tell me now."

"I lied to you." She said.

"I am in a forgiving mood. What did you lie about?" He asked her as he moved closer to her.

"My parents. The people you met were not my parents."

She said.

He was shocked. "Is this another joke like the circus dwarf?"

"No. I'm standing here crying, and you think I am joking. What is wrong with you?" She turned away from him.

Jacob went up to stand behind her and put his arms around her. He put his face on her shoulder. "Amelia, stop fighting with me. I love you. I'm just surprised that you went through all that trouble to introduce me to two people and pass them off as your parents. I forgive you for lying to me, but I want to understand why you thought you had to."

"I am illegitimate. My father never married my mother." She told him.

"That doesn't have to be common knowledge. We can keep that between us. It doesn't change the fact that I love you. Can I meet your mother?" He asked her.

"No. She died years ago. The two people you met took me in for a few years. My mother left them money to take care of me. When the money ran out they put me out. It was the job here that saved me from living on the street. I paid them to pretend to be my parents." She told him.

"Do you know who your father is?" Jacob asked.

"I never met him, but he sent my mother money to take care of me until she died. After that I never saw another penny." I told him. "He knows who I am, but I don't know who he is. I knew she was threatening to expose him and that is why he sent her money. If he should appear one day and tell me that I am his daughter, I will not know if it is the truth. She never told me who he was. She never told me anything about him. Jacob, you don't know what you are getting when you marry me. I could be contaminated somehow."

He turned her around and put his arms around her to hold her affectionately. "Amelia, you are not contaminated. You are precious and wonderful. You have a beautiful smile, and you make me laugh. I adore you. I don't care if your father is the King of France or a man in prison. He had his chance to find out how wonderful you are and he lost it. I promise to protect your secret. We will be married, and I will be your family along with Olivia, Keith, Charles and Duke Chalon. We will not fight about anything else in this marriage. We will talk to each other in English. I cannot keep up with you when you speak French so quickly."

"When are we getting married?" She asked him.

"Two weeks. The cottage will be completed by then." He told her.

She looked up at him and smiled.

He let go of her. "You behave. We are in the Duke's house and his mother is on this floor. Two weeks and I can satisfy that gleam in your eyes."

"That is why I love you so much. You could have easily taken advantage of my attraction for you, but each time, you chose to be honorable toward me. Your love for me is amazing." Amelia said and then she kissed him.

"Come downstairs and talk with Olivia and me about the

wedding. I will meet you downstairs." Jacob turned the key in the lock and put the key in his pocket. Then he left the room.

When Amelia came out of her room, Lady Jacqueline was standing outside her door. "Can I help you, Lady Jacqueline?"

"Why did you have a man in your bedroom Amelia?" She had an accusing tone.

"My fiancé was in my bedroom to talk to me about something privately." She answered.

"How many times have you invited him into your room for a private talk?" Lady Jacqueline asked her using the same tone of voice.

"I have never invited him into my room." Amelia replied.

"Then how did he manage to get in?" She asked.

"With a key. Why don't we go downstairs together? He is discussing our wedding plans with the Duchess. I'm sure he can explain to you where he got the key and why he chose to use it." Amelia said.

Lady Jacqueline wasn't backing off. "Yes, let's do that."

Amelia led the way to the dining room. She found me there with Jacob. "Lady Jacqueline saw you coming out of my room and she has some questions for you, Jacob."

"Amelia tells me that she did not invite you into her room." She said.

"That is correct." Jacob answered.

"Where did you get the key to her room?" Lady Jacqueline asked.

"The Duke told me where to find it and advised me to use it. I took his advice and entered Amelia's room uninvited. We had a very private discussion about our upcoming wedding and future marriage. The Duke's advice proved to be just what we needed to solve the issues we were facing." Jacob answered. "In case you were wondering, Amelia is a fine woman whom I love and respect. She has never done anything to be ashamed of or feel guilty about, nor have I."

"Thank you for your time." Lady Jacqueline turned and left the room.

Jacob hugged Amelia. "Don't let her bother you." He kissed her on the top of the head. "Come and help us plan the wedding."

She took his hand, and they joined me at the table to continue the discussion.

Two weeks later, Amelia and Jacob were married by a minister as family and close friends looked on. They enjoyed a few days of privacy before returning to work. During the day, Amelia would play little practical jokes on Jacob just to keep him laughing.

One day she walked up to him as he was standing in the hall. She stuffed something quickly into his pocket and whispered, "Jacob, these are too tight and I have nowhere to put them." Then she disappeared quickly around the corner.

He suspected her of something devious. He looked up and

down the hall to make sure no one was around. When he was sure not to be discovered, he pulled the item out of his pocket discreetly. He cracked up laughing when he realized it was a very large woman's panties. He stuffed them back into his pocket until he could find a way to get rid of them.

Paul came to bed with stories that Jacob had told him about Amelia's practical jokes.

"She is a joy to me also. When we are not working I am laughing with her." I told Paul.

"She put love notes to him in his shoes in the morning. She found a way to get a note inside a muffin the other morning. He almost choked on it. She entices him all day long with her plans and jokes. I wonder how long this will last. I think he falls more deeply in love with her each day." Paul told me. "I see him looking for her like a lost puppy."

"I hope Keith and Charles find someone as fascinating as Amelia."

"Rumor suggests that Charles is sweet on Yvette Volcy. She is nearly his age and has never been married. He remarked that he wouldn't mind being with a plain girl. She's very nice but her features are not extraordinary. Her father would jump at the chance to have her marry Charles." He told me.

Chapter Thirteen

"Mr. Volcy, I would like your permission to ask your daughter Yvette to be my wife." Charles said to him.

"Yes, Mr. Douglas you have my blessing." Mr. Volcy told him.

Charles smiled and went right outside to interrupt Yvette's time in the garden. She was working on the roses she had been attending for a month.

"Yvette." Charles said as he approached her.

She pricked her finger on a torn. "Ouch."

"I'm sorry. I didn't mean to startle you." Charles apologized.

"I'm fine. I did not expect to see you today Charles. I am a frightful mess." She apologized.

"You look lovely to me." He said.

"You always seem to have the right words for me. Is there something I can help you with?" She asked.

"Yvette, I know we haven't known each other very long, but I find you are an amazing woman. I have spoken with your father just now. Yvette, would you consider my offer and consent to take me as your husband? I would very much like to marry you."

She stared at him. "Charles, are you sure you want me as your wife?"

"Yes, of course I am. I wouldn't have asked you if I wasn't sure." He replied.

"But you could have any beautiful woman you wanted in France. You're quite handsome. There is nothing special about me. I've never been noticed by any man before. You and I have only talked about plants and matters of business. I have not felt any romantic intentions from you. This comes as a complete surprise." She said.

"It is true that our conversations haven't had a lot of romantic substance. I am very attracted to you, Yvette. You are sweet and smart. You are unassuming and humble. All of these are qualities I admire about you. I have avoided the romantic part of our relationship because I would be too tempted to act on it. I wanted to respect you and treat you honorably. Don't say that you are not beautiful or that I would prefer someone else. That is not true. You are beautiful to me, and I do want to marry you if you will have me." He said.

"If I said yes, when were you planning on having this wedding?" She asked him.

"As soon as possible. I'm not a young man by today's standards." He said.

"How old are you?" She asked.

"Twenty-eight." He answered.

"No, you are too old for me. Wrinkles will be creeping into your face in moments." She smiled.

"Yvette, please don't torture me. Tell me that you will marry me." Charles pleaded.

"If you want me, I'm yours." She said.

"Do you love me, Yvette?" He asked.

"I didn't dare to feel love for you, Charles, because I thought you would just visit with me a few more times and move on to someone else. I want to love you. To be honest, I am afraid that you will become bored with me very soon after we are married and want someone else more suited to you. I say yes in fear of that." She told him.

"I will plan to marry you in a month. In that time I intend to prove to your heart that I am worthy of your love and affection. I will not look to another woman for the things in our life that we share so completely. I won't hurt you like that. You have my word." He said.

"Alright, Charles. I will open my heart to loving you." She said.

"May I kiss you, Yvette?" He asked.

"Charles, I'm a complete mess." She was astonished he would ask.

"Not to me." He said as he approached her.

"I consent to the kiss, but I warn you I have not experienced this before." She said as she looked up at him.

"We will take it slow." He put his hands on her waist and leaned toward her and kissed her lips. "You are a little nervous about this aren't you?"

"Yes." She answered.

"Close your eyes Yvette and let's try this again."

With her eyes closed she waited for the touch of his lips. It didn't take her long to understand the romance of his kiss and how to respond to it.

"Is my heart supposed to race like this?" She asked innocently.

He put her hand on his chest. "Can you feel my heart beat?"

"Yes."

"Kiss me again and keep your hand there." He told her.

She did and got lost in the romance of it. "Charles, this is a wonderful experience. I don't think it will take much time at all to know I am in love with you."

He smiled. "I could not adore you more. Let's go tell your father that you have accepted my proposal." He took her hand and walked with her into her home.

Her parents were overjoyed that their daughter was finally getting married. The next day, they had a celebration with their closest friends to announce the good news. They introduced Charles as their future son-in-law. Charles learned later that day that Yvette came with quite a sizable dowry. He talked it over with Yvette.

"I don't need the money or the items of your dowry, but I will take them out of respect for your father. As soon as we are married, all that money will be put into a trust for you. You can draw on it any time you want to without asking for permission from anyone. If you want to save it, save it. If you want to spend it, spend it. It is yours completely." He told her.

"Well, that answers another prayer." She replied.

"Prayer about what?" He asked.

"I am plain Charles. Most men expect a sizable dowry for marrying a plain girl. Now I know you really love me and want to marry me for me." She said.

"From now on you will not refer to yourself as plain. I forbid it. You will tell everyone that your husband believes you are beautiful, so therefore, you are." He insisted.

She wiggled her finger to have him come closer to her. Then she whispered, "Kiss me."

He smiled and did as she requested.

A month later, we attended their wedding at Mr. Volcy's estate. Charles and Yvette looked very happy and they received a great variety of wedding gifts. Charles watched over Yvette and was very protective of the way people treated her. He pampered her as often as he could. He was right about her; she was an extraordinary woman who had a fine sense of humor. It was apparent to everyone who saw them together that they loved each other very much.

Olivia's Story

A month later, Amelia was showing signs of being pregnant. She was tired and nauseated most of the time. Jacob insisted that she stay in the cottage and rest. We agreed with him.

Lady Jacqueline was becoming more and more concerned that I was not pregnant. She pressured Paul to have a doctor check me out, but he refused to bother me with her concerns. She became frustrated and spoke directly to me.

"Olivia, may I speak with you?" She asked me as I entered the sitting room.

"Certainly. How can I help you?" I asked her.

"Olivia, I am concerned for you, my dear." She said.

"I assure you I feel fine, and I am happy." I told her.

"Paul is anxious to be able to enjoy his children. You have been married over a year now, and still you have not been able to get pregnant. Please have the doctor check you. Maybe there is something simple he could recommend to you that would help you to conceive a child for Paul." She said.

I laughed to keep myself from slapping her.

"I do not understand what is so funny." She seemed insulted.

"The problem is not with me, Lady Jacqueline. The problem is with your son. I've kept it a secret because frankly it is none of your business; but if you want to discuss it with him, go right ahead. I'm sure it will embarrass and humiliate him to have his mother talk to him about male issues." I whispered.

"Oh my!" She was surprised.

"We may never have a child. You should just appreciate the grandchildren you have. I love my husband and I know he would appreciate it if you did not mention this to anyone else. I'm sure he would be very upset if he found out you told others." I warned her.

"Oh, I would never." She promised and left me.

That night I told Paul about my conversation with his mother.

"I cannot believe you told my own mother that lie." He was a little upset with me.

"Well, how dare she speak to me that way. She has no right sticking her nose into our marriage." I told him.

"So this is what you do to keep her out of it? That was an evil thing to say about me. Is this how you honor your husband?"

"All this time you and your mother have found fault with me. What if it is you? We don't know about the dynamics of the human body." I told him.

He forced himself to be reasonable. "Before we go blaming each other, why don't we just pray about it? We can ask God to bless us according to Deuteronomy 28; the fruit of your womb will be blessed. God can be responsible for this and we can both relax. Don't bring this up again. Avoid the conversation with her." He insisted.

"That is a very good idea. Let's pray." I agreed.

Paul held my hands in his and he prayed for our marriage

and our future family claiming the blessing of God over my womb. Then he kissed me.

I was pregnant in a few weeks. I tried my best to hide it from him and his mother. It wasn't too difficult because I wasn't nearly as sick as Amelia. My stomach felt queasy only in the evening when I was tired.

Paul woke up in the middle of the night as I was standing near the window breathing deeply trying to settle my stomach.

"Olivia? Close the window. It's getting too cool in here." He said.

"I need the fresh air." I told him.

He got up and threw a blanket over me. "Your arms are cold. Come to bed." He tried to get me to move.

"No, not yet. I need this." I insisted.

"You need to be chilled and breathe cold air? Come to bed." He insisted.

"Alright." I gave in and started back to bed and fainted.

He picked me up and put me in the bed. "Olivia, wake up!"

I came around almost immediately. "I'm alright. Relax Paul."

"You're not alright. I'm sending for the doctor." He insisted as he started for the door.

"Paul, please come to bed. If I don't feel well in the morning, I will not object to sending for the doctor. Please come to bed and keep me warm." I told him.

"Alright, but in the morning if you are no better I call for the doctor." He insisted as he climbed into bed and put his arm under my neck. He drew me close to him.

"Paul, I know I will be fine." I told him.

"What if you had fainted right out the window? If you don't feel well, wake me up and tell me." He said.

"You would be getting up quite a bit then." I told him.

"You mean you haven't been feeling well, and you've kept it from me?" He was concerned.

"I wanted to be sure first." I told him.

"Sure you were sick?" He asked.

"No, sure I was pregnant." I smiled up at him.

"Pregnant? Are you pregnant?" He asked.

"Yes, at least a few months." I told him.

"Olivia, how could you keep this a secret from me for so long? You know how much I want to have a baby."

"I just wanted to be sure. I didn't want to get your hopes up and then have it be a mistake." I rolled away from him and ran to the window and opened it again to breathe in the cold air.

He got up quickly and covered me with a blanket. Then he pulled a chair over to the window. He put a blanket on it for himself, sat down and held me in his lap covering us both. I put my head on his shoulder as he held me close.

"This is better." I told him.

"You rest. I'll hold you until you feel better or fall asleep." He said.

I kissed him on the cheek. "Thank you, honey."

When I fell asleep in his arms, he carried me to the bed and put me in it. Then he covered us up and fell asleep beside me. I was so tired in the morning that he just let me sleep. He went into his office after breakfast and started the morning work with Jacob. The weather was so nice outside that he opened the windows of his office.

"Fire! Fire!" They heard the servants yelling.

His mother was running down the staircase. "Paul, the vineyard is in flames!"

He ran outside with Jacob. He started yelling for every man to help them.

"Come with me! There is no saving the north vineyard. Let's concentrate on wetting down the south." They ran in the direction of the water barrels.

Lady Jacqueline ordered all the female servants to strip every bed and bring every blanket down to the men. "Soak them with water and bring them down to the men to throw over the plants."

I woke up to the frantic sounds of many people yelling. I put on my robe as the servants knocked on my door.

"Duchess, we need every sheet and blanket. We must soak them and bring them to the Duke." One of our servants told

me.

"Do it!" I told them as I rushed to get dressed.

The smoke was seen for miles. Charles and Keith got on their horses and raced to help us.

Amelia was running out the door to help when Keith got to the front of the house. He jumped off his horse and chased her. He stopped her. "You are not going near that fire. You are carrying a child. I order you to stay here." He insisted.

"Jacob is out there." She said.

"I know. He is with Paul. Go in the house and pray for their safety. Now, go back. You will only distract him and that will cause him injury." Keith ordered her.

"Keith is right. We would only get in the way and distract them with our presence." I told her as we watched from the front of the house. "We must trust in the Lord for their safety."

We prayed together that God would intervene for us and keep those who were fighting the fire safe.

Our neighbors and friends started to show up with more people to help. The men ran leaving their horses and carriages at the front of the house. Some of them went toward the vineyard while others went to the stable to bring the horses out just in case the fire switched direction.

The smoke started to move toward the house.

"Amelia, help me to close the windows, or our home will be filled with smoke." I ran back into the house.

Some of our female servants were returning. As they did Lady Jacqueline sent them to the rooms to help us. As we were closing the last of the windows, it started to rain. I got down on my knees and thanked God for helping us.

When the fire was out, Paul returned to the house with Jacob, Charles and Keith. Our neighbors and friends followed him into the mansion. He ordered the staff in the house to bring everyone something to eat and drink. Each of them smelled of smoke. Their faces and hands were dirty. A few had ripped shirts.

I went to him and hugged him. "I'm so glad you are safe."

"We were all very fortunate. The rain is taking care of everything that was smoldering. This was not an accident. Fire just doesn't start on a mild day like today. I will find out who did this to us, and they will be punished." He was overheard by everyone standing near us.

"How much did we lose?" I asked him.

"Not as much as I feared we would. There was no wind to blow the fire. Everyone put in a great effort to contain it to the north vineyard. The south vineyard was not touched. I have men in the fields now. As soon as everyone here is taken care of I want food and drink sent to those working in the fields." He said.

"I'll see to it for you." I told him.

"Olivia, give the order to Amelia. Let her find a way to carry it out." Paul instructed me. "I want you by my side."

"Alright." I left him for a moment and told Amelia what he

wanted.

She went into the kitchen right away and gave direction to the servants. Jacob was not bothered by this, but Keith was although he kept it to himself.

Keith met Amelia as she was coming out of the kitchen. "How have you been feeling?"

"Rather well now. I think the morning sickness has passed. Jacob and I take a short walk each night so that I can get some exercise. We love to talk in the peacefulness of walking alone together." She looked at her husband. "I love him so very much."

"I know you do. It shows when you look at him." Keith said.

"Why do you still work?" Keith asked. "Certainly Jacob can afford to have you stay home."

"I do it to be around the Duchess. I have been teaching her French. She is more of a friend than a Duchess to me." I whispered to him.

"Oh, so this job is a pleasure to you?" He smiled.

"Yes. I love this family. All of you are in my heart." Amelia told him.

"I've never met anyone like you, Amelia. Jacob is a very fortunate man to have found you." Keith said.

"What a wonderful compliment. Thank you. Please excuse me. I have to report back to the Duchess." She left him.

Charles came to join Keith. He whispered. "Be careful,

brother. Your love for your brother's wife shows in your eyes. You should find someone who is just yours to love alone."

"You assume to know too much." Keith told him. "We should leave. I know I need a bath."

Charles and Keith slipped out and went home. Paul said goodbye and thanked all the people who had come to help that day. As the sheets and blankets were returned to the house, the servants made a valiant effort to get them washed. We set up two rooms on the main floor to hang them up to dry. Jacob rigged up ropes from one side of the room to the other. It rained all night and into the next day, but it wasn't a heavy rain.

The next day, Paul went out with Jacob to inspect the damage. "This will cut into our profits, but it won't ruin us. God was good to us." He told Jacob.

"Yes. He was." Jacob agreed.

"Send an invitation out to Keith and Charles to join us tonight for supper. Tell Charles to bring Yvette and Keith is welcome to bring a guest if he likes. Supper will be just before sunset. Send an invitation to Andre and Philippe and their families. I also wish to invite Duchess Dupree." Paul instructed him.

"I'll send a message to each of them as soon as we return to the office." Jacob told him.

During supper that night, Paul announced my pregnancy. Everyone, especially his mother, was overwhelmed with joy about the news. When the excitement died down he informed everyone of the damage to the vineyard and what it would mean in terms of profit. We were relieved that the news was not as bad as we thought it might be. The rest of the evening we enjoyed the company of our extended family. There was much laughter and light-hearted conversation. At the end of the evening, my mother invited me to a luncheon the next day. She was entertaining some close friends and wanted me to be part of it with Amelia. I accepted the invitation. She extended the invitation to her good friend Lady Jacqueline, but she politely declined. She had already made other plans. Then she turned to Yvette who was delighted to be invited.

Everyone left together. The moon was full. That made me feel better about their safety going home.

"Paul, do you think the person who set fire to the vineyard will try again?" I asked him.

"I hope not, but I am taking precautions. I have hired men to stay awake and protect the vineyard. In all things we must trust God. No weapon formed against us will prosper. That is what His word says and that is what I believe." He told me. "Now come with me. We must tuck you in and make sure you rest."

"I hope you are not going to neglect us just because I am carrying your child. I don't need a father. I need a husband." I told him.

"I could not neglect you even if I wanted to. Your heart draws me to you. I cannot resist your enticing ways." He whispered.

I laughed at his words.

"Why do you laugh? Each night you lure me into your arms. I have tried to resist you in order to rest, but you will not hear of it. Am I not telling the truth?" He said seriously.

"No, you are not telling the truth." I laughed. We were passing his mother on the steps, and I could tell she wanted to eavesdrop on our conversation. "Paul, I am so relieved that your particular problem did not prevent us from conceiving this child." I said it loud enough so she could hear me, but soft enough so that it would not sound like I wanted her to.

He stopped me on the steps and put his arms around me. "Excuse us, Mother." He said as she was about to pass. He kissed me over and over again until I begged him to take me to our room. "I can't yet. You have embarrassed me for the last time." I felt his hands move and his anger with them. He didn't care who was walking by.

"Paul please. You are embarrassing me in front of the servants." I begged him to stop.

He stopped and stared at me. "You will correct the misconception my mother has about me; or next time, the staircase may be our bed. Do you understand me? This is no longer amusing to me." He was serious.

"I'm sorry. You are right. My comments did not honor you and it is no longer a joke. Let me go, and I will apologize to her for misleading her about you. I'm very sorry." I apologized.

"I'll meet you in our room." He said as he walked away from me. He was still angry.

I hurried down the staircase and met his mother as she was

entering the sitting room to pick up her knitting. "Lady Jacqueline, may I speak with you?"

"Certainly Olivia." She said.

"I owe you an apology. I lied to you about Paul's condition." I admitted.

"Why would you do that?" She asked.

"I was angry that there was so much pressure on me to become pregnant. I just wanted to shift the blame to him so that you would stop pressuring us. Then on the staircase, I was just being inconsiderate to you and to him. He is quite upset with me for lying, and I don't blame him. Please forgive me. I'm very sorry."

"So there is no problem?" She wanted to make sure.

"I made the entire thing up. There was no substance of truth in it." I told her.

"You are forgiven. If I should put my nose into your business again, please tactfully tell me to mind my own business. I will remember this conversation and do my best not to intrude into your personal matters. I have learned my lesson also. Goodnight, Olivia." She said.

"Goodnight." I went upstairs to my husband and slowly entered the room. "Are you still angry with me?"

"Did you clear things up with my mother?" He asked.

"Yes. I told her that I lied to her, and I explained why I did it. I told her that the remark on the steps was inconsiderate of you and her, and I asked her to forgive me." I explained. "Paul,

I am very sorry. I was playing a child's game at your expense. It will not happen again. I promise."

"Go to bed, Olivia. I'm going for a walk to clear my head and my heart." He told me. Then he walked out the door.

I was asleep when he came back into our bedroom. He climbed into bed next to me and fell asleep. In the morning he was up before me. I heard he was in the vineyard while I was getting dressed. I looked out the window, but I didn't see him. I never got the chance to speak to him before Amelia and I left to go to my mother's luncheon.

"Paul, what are we doing in this tavern?" Jacob asked him.

"Trying to get information. Just keep your ears open." Paul told him.

The bar maids were quick to flock to their table. Paul asked a few questions and ordered drinks for them. A few of the women were paying extra attention to Paul when they brought the flow of drinks to the table.

"Paul, what are you doing?" Jacob asked him.

"I told you. I am looking for information." He said.

"Excuse me, Duke Chalon, but it looks as if you are looking for more than information. Have you forgotten that you are married to my sister?" Jacob was clearly upset with him.

"This is harmless attention, Jacob." Paul insisted.

The girls came to him again and kissed him on the cheek when they put the drinks down.

"I'm leaving. Are you coming or not?" Jacob told him.

"Not." Paul said. "Remember, you work for me."

"Not at the expense of my sister's honor." Jacob got up and punched him in the face. "I quit!"

That strike started a fight in the tavern.

We were coming back from my mother's luncheon when a carriage sped by us.

"It looked like the Duke was in the carriage with Jacob and another man." Amelia said. "Why would they be traveling that fast? Do you think there is another fire?"

"I hope not. Can we get the driver to speed up?" I asked her.

"No. I don't think so. We are enclosed. With the sound of the horses traveling, he won't hear us." Amelia said.

When we got to the mansion a servant came out to meet us. "Miss Amelia, come quickly. Your husband is injured."

Amelia ran into the mansion and I was right behind her.

"Where is my husband?" She asked the servant.

"They carried him upstairs to the room he used to have. The doctor is with him." The servant replied.

"Send for Keith Chalon and Charles Douglas at once. Tell them to come here." I told the servant. Then I followed Amelia upstairs. We barged into the room and all we saw was blood. The doctor got up and left the side of Jacob's bed.

"I've done what I can, Duke Chalon. He's lost a lot of blood and there is damage I cannot repair." He whispered to Paul.

I saw the evidence of kisses on Paul's cheeks and could smell the liquor as Amelia went to sit beside her husband. I rushed to be beside my brother.

"Jacob, my love, don't leave me. We have a child who needs to be held in his father's arms." She cried.

"I'm sorry, Amelia. I would not leave you if I had a choice in this." He struggled to speak to her through the pain. "I held on just to see your face one last time."

"Jacob, hold on to life. Fight to stay with us." I wept as I held his hand from the other side of the bed.

"Please stay with me." Amelia wept.

"I will love you forever, Amelia. I will be the angel who watches over our child." He put his hand on the side of her face for a moment. Then it dropped as he started gasping for air.

I watched in horror knowing I was helpless to help him.

"Jacob! Jacob! Stay with us! Please. I'm begging you." She watched him die. "No. You have to come back to me. Please, Jacob. Please come back to me." She wept on his chest as she held on to him. "Please come back. Please. Please come back."

I was crying with her. We refused to leave his side. Keith and Charles ran into the room and saw him lying on the bed. They heard us crying in agony as Paul stood in the corner crying.

Charles came to me and Keith went to Amelia. They gently coaxed us away from Jacob to lead us out of the room.

"How did this happen? How could I lose the one person I love most in this world?" She continued to weep as she stood up. Her dress was stained with his blood.

"I don't know. Come away with me, Amelia. Let them take care of Jacob." Keith had tears in his eyes as he took her out into the hallway.

I watched tears fall from my husband's eyes as he stood near the bed. He said nothing. He just stared at Jacob as we left the room.

"Keith, bring Amelia to my room." I told him.

"Amelia, we will stay with you." Keith said as they climbed the stairs together.

"Please find out how this happened. I need to know what happened and why." She said through her tears.

Tears flowed down his cheeks. "I will find out. I will be back to tell you after I know you are resting in Olivia's room." He promised as he wiped the tears from his cheeks.

"Olivia, who was with Jacob when this happened?" Charles asked as we entered my room.

"He was with Paul." I answered him.

"I'll talk to him." Keith put Amelia on my bed. "I'll send someone to get clothes for you to change into." He told her.

"No, not now. Just find out what happened." She was insistent.

He kissed her on the forehead. "I promise I will find out. Charles stay with them." Keith left the room.

Keith looked for Paul and couldn't find him. He had left Jacob. He checked with the servants. They pointed him to the cottage that Jacob and Amelia had shared together. He found Paul in the bedroom going through Jacob's clothes to pick something out for his funeral.

"What are you doing here? Your wife and Amelia are upstairs. You should be with them." Keith said as he walked in on Paul.

When Paul turned around, Keith saw the lipstick marks on his cheeks.

"Did Olivia see the evidence of other women on your face?" Keith asked.

Paul just realized how many people had seen the evidence of his indulgences. "I'm a fool."

"I'm not arguing that point with you now. Stop what you are doing and tell me what happened."

"Not now." Paul kept looking through Jacob's clothes.

Keith grabbed him by the arm and pulled him to a chair. "Sit down! There is a devastated widow wearing a bloody dress crying over the husband she just lost. She sent me to find out why he died, and I want to know why. You seem to be the only one with answers, so start talking!"

Paul started to cry. He was grief stricken. "It's my fault."

"I'll wait for more information. We are not leaving this cottage until I know everything. My brother died today. I want an explanation." Keith demanded.

It was ten minutes before Paul started to explain. When he was done telling his story Keith asked him, "What are you leaving out of the story?"

"What do you mean?"

"All the time I've known you, I haven't felt that you have been completely honest. You prove it over and over again with so many things. There is always a hidden agenda with you, Paul. You are this nice caring guy on the surface. You breathe out charm and sophistication, but down to earth honest is not you. I believe you hold some responsibility today for what happened, but you didn't hold the knife that killed Jacob. You want to lie to me, that's fine. You want to lie to yourself, go right ahead. But let me give you a good piece of advice. Whatever you are trying to hide will eat at you until there is no good left in you. Start being honest with yourself and Olivia. Be honest with God. He knows anyway. You aren't hiding anything from him." Keith got up and left him. He returned to my bedroom. He went to talk to Amelia. "Amelia sweetheart, come take a walk with me. I'll tell you what you want to know."

She got off the bed and took his hand.

"Keith, tell us all." I stopped him at the door.

"Paul needs to talk to you Olivia. I'll tell Charles after I talk to Amelia." Keith told me. He opened the door and escorted her outside toward her cottage. He didn't intend to take her there. He just wanted to walk in that area because it was more private.

"Tell me." She said.

"Paul took Jacob with him to the tavern. Paul said they went there to see if they could find out information that might lead them to discover who set fire to the vineyard. According to Paul, some of the men in the bar knew who he was and stayed away out of respect for him. The barmaids brought the drinks. As Paul was trying to obtain information from them he let them get a little too affectionate with him. Jacob was concerned for Olivia and asked Paul to leave with him. Paul refused and reminded Jacob about his job and who he worked for. Jacob punched Paul in the face and quit his job. That started the fight at the tavern and everyone was in on it. In the midst of the fight someone pulled a knife and stabbed Jacob. No one saw it happen. No one knows who did it, not even Paul." Keith explained.

"He loved Olivia so much. He told me that they had a special bond. I can see him being furious with Paul about his actions. He was a man of honor and integrity. Paul's disregard for his wife and marriage led to this and brought death to my husband. It is so unfair to us and to our child. How can I stay here? How can I survive here knowing that he is responsible?" She asked him.

"Amelia, pack your things. I've bought a place that is big enough for you to have your own room and a room for the baby. I will take care of you and the baby. You won't have to work another day. It will be my gift to my brother to make sure that you will survive well with his child. Please consider my offer." Keith said.

"You love me, don't you?" She asked.

He hesitated to answer her. "This isn't the right time to ask or to answer such a question."

"It is the right time. I have nothing left and I need to know the truth about how you feel." She said.

"Amelia, there are no conditions in regard to you moving into my home. I will honor you now and in the future. I respect you. I had great respect for my brother and his love for you. All I want to do right now is help you and the baby you are carrying. You are hurt right now. Let's not discuss anything that might upset you more. Give yourself time to heal from this." He said.

"You are right. I need time. All my thoughts are jumbled up together, and I'm not thinking clearly. After the funeral, please help me to move out of the cottage and away from the Duke." She said.

"I will help you in any way that I can. You can count on me Amelia. I will not let you down." Keith promised.

"Thank you. Will you take me back to my cottage? I need to change and have some time alone." She said.

"Are you sure you want to be alone?" He asked her.

"Yes. My husband's presence is in that cottage. His pillow is on our bed. I need those things near me and I need to be alone loving and thinking about him." She said as tears flowed down her cheeks.

"Alright Amelia. If you need me, send someone to get me. I don't care what time it is. I will come. I promise." He said.

"You're very kind, Keith. Thank you. I know how hurt you are by all of this. Jacob loved you very much, and I know you loved him." She walked with him to the cottage. Paul had already left. She went in alone and locked the door.

Keith came back to speak with Charles and check on the funeral arrangements for the next day. Charles was coming down the stairs to meet him.

"Paul is speaking with Olivia. The funeral is scheduled for ten in the morning at the church. Let's go Keith. You can tell me what happened when we get to my house. Staying here will not help us right now." Charles looked devastated.

They left the house.

"Olivia, I'm sorry. I didn't mean for any of this to happen." He apologized.

"Be honest with me, Paul. You allowed those women to kiss you because of me. It wasn't the information you were seeking. You wanted to feel like a man, and I crushed that between us by my comments about your abilities in our bedroom. No one else knows, but I do. It's my fault. I joked about your manhood, and you wanted to prove to yourself that you were a desirable man. I caused you to betray us and I caused my brother's death. There is no forgiveness for me now." I ran from the room and down the staircase, and he chased me.

"Olivia! Stop." He ran after me and was surprised that he lost me. "Search the house and the grounds for the Duchess. She is overcome with grief. We must find her. No matter what she says, find me and tell me where she is." He gave orders to his servants.

Lady Jacqueline saw Paul in the front hallway. "Paul, take a breath and settle your mind. Think about this for a minute. What did she say and where would she go?"

He paced the floor for a minute. "The church. She could get there by running through the woods."

"Go. If anyone finds her elsewhere, I will send them to you and I will go to her myself until you reach us." His mother assured him.

"Be kind to her. She is beside herself with grief." Paul told her.

"Of course. Go Paul. Find her." His mother encouraged him.

He ran out the back door and through the woods toward the church. He got to the church and went inside. He found me on the floor in front of the altar weeping and asking for forgiveness as the Pastor knelt down next to me. It broke his heart. As he approached me, the Pastor got up and left us.

"Olivia, please stop this. You are not to blame in any of this." He picked me up from the floor to stand in front of him. Then he put his arms around me and held me close while I cried.

"I shouldn't have said those things about you to your mother. I shouldn't have joked and made you resent me. Words have power, and I used mine for evil and now my brother is dead." I cried.

"Olivia, that is not true. Not any of it. It was a joke on my mother. God knew you did not mean it as evil. He understood your heart. God judges the heart. Your heart could not cause me to act against you. I did that because I was being stupid and prideful. I need your forgiveness. You don't need mine or God's or anyone's in this matter. You did nothing wrong. You apologized, and I should have put my pride away and just forgiven you for offending me. I treated you badly on the staircase. I threatened you. I was wrong in all of this, but I excused my own behavior against you. I acted in the greatest of error and caused your brother to despise my actions. He had a perfect right to punch me in the face. I deserved it. It is just that everyone was drinking in the tavern. We all had too much and lost sense of who we were and what was really happening. An evil man killed your brother. An evil man took out a knife and killed him. People make choices every day, Olivia. That man chose to kill, and Jacob was the one who happened to be there. He was going to kill someone. Evil does that. You are not evil Olivia. You are not guilty of any of it. Please believe me. Please don't let evil win and persuade you that you are guilty of something when you are not. I love you, Olivia. I swear to you that I will never let my pride hurt us again. I wish I could take my actions back and change what happened, but I can't. Please forgive me for my part in your sorrow and Jacob's death."

"Take me home." I told him.

We walked back to the mansion through the woods as he continued to console me. He took me up to our room and helped me change. Then he tucked me in bed and let me rest. We didn't speak about anything else. He went downstairs to check on the funeral arrangements for Jacob.

"How is she?" His mother asked him.

"Resting and crying." He answered.

"Paul, I'm your mother. I love you. You can talk to me about anything, and it will remain between us." She promised.

"Keith accused me of not being honest with myself about who I am. He said I was hiding something. He accused me of always having an agenda when I deal with people. Those words haunt me. I've been thinking about them. Upstairs is the sweetest, most amazing person I know, and today I betrayed her. I pushed guilt out of my mind and let other women kiss me and flatter me, and I enjoyed it while it was happening. I had little regard for Olivia or my marriage. I could blame it on the drinks or my wounded pride, but neither is a good enough excuse. I felt I was entitled to disregard her. How could I be that man and then this one who loves her so completely?"

"I don't know. Love is a choice, Paul. We choose it each day. You have to ask yourself why you hated Olivia today." She said.

"Hate? Is that what you think I did?" He asked her.

"That is exactly what you did. I am not going to sweeten this up for you. You know me better than that. At the moment you disregarded your vows to her, you despised her. In your heart, you hated her. Your actions were motivated by hate." She said.

"That is a hard thing to accept, Mother, in the midst of all this." He replied.

"Paul, you have a spirit of entitlement. You justify every deal and every bargain you've made at the expense of others so that you can achieve the success to which you believe you are entitled. Even when Marita died, your prayers were prayers of entitlement. You used phrases like she deserves, I deserve, haven't we done enough for You. Your position in this community does not keep you humble. You speak to servants a certain way because you believe you are entitled to do so. You treat your wife a certain way because you believe you are entitled to. Even when Jacob put you in your place, your reaction was to remind him that he worked for you. Start being honest with yourself, Paul. I think you were attracted to Olivia because she is innocent, sweet and young. She loves you beyond herself. I saw that today. She was willing to take the blame for your behavior and her brother's death. I'm not sure she believed she was responsible. I am sure she believed you could not accept your own responsibility for what happened. Not initially anyway. If you want to be honest with yourself, look at your actions over time. Does the end truly justify the means?" She asked.

"It seems I lost quite a bit trying to justify my actions." He admitted.

"If your wife invites you back into her bed after this, you are one very blessed man. Honor her, Paul. In everything you do and say, honor her." His mother said and then she left him.

He came back to our room about an hour later. I was asleep in the bed. He felt guilty about climbing into bed with me so he sat in the chair beside the bed and fell asleep.

I woke up in the middle of the night. I saw him sitting in the chair sleeping. I got up and knelt beside him. "Paul."

He opened his eyes and looked down at me. That bothered him. "Olivia, you should be sleeping."

"Why are you sleeping in this chair?" I asked him.

"I didn't want to disturb you." He said.

I stood up and sat in his lap, putting my arms around his neck. I kissed him and immediately tears flowed from his eyes. "Paul, is it sorrow that causes your tears?"

"No, Olivia, it is your forgiveness that affects me. I don't deserve it." He said.

"I don't give it because you deserve it. I give it because I love you and I am not willing to give you up." I told him.

"I wish I knew how to love you like you love me." He said.

"Come to bed, Paul. We will need each other more than ever these next few days. Hold on to me. Don't leave me to my own imagination. I need your voice and your touch." I told him.

He climbed into bed beside me and held me close to him. We fell asleep in each other's arms.

Chapter Fourteen

Amelia wasn't so forgiving. After the funeral she moved into Keith's estate. He gave her a private sitting room and two bedrooms of her own. He explained to her that he would not enter her section of the manor unless she invited him. The rest of the manor they shared with the exception of his bedroom.

Amelia wasn't herself for months. She kept to herself most of the time. The only thing she did seem to enjoy was needlework, knitting and crocheting.

"Your baby will be here soon." Keith remarked as they ate supper together.

"It seems like yesterday that you brought me here. I have trouble believing it's been six months already. You are right. The little one already keeps me up at night. It is close to the time for him or her to make an entrance into our world. There is no way to tell if I will have a good baby or one who keeps me up at night." She replied.

"Amelia, there was a light in you that is so dim now I hardly recognize you. Isn't there a chance of joy returning to you somehow? Jacob loved the Amelia who was with him. He would want you to be that same Amelia for your child." He told her.

"I feel like if I laugh or joke, I have forgotten the tragedy of his death. I feel like I am betraying his memory. I am supposed to mourn for him." She explained.

He reached for her hand and put his over it. "Amelia, Jacob is with God. There is no sorrow in heaven. He has no pain. He will get no older. He lives in a mansion and listens from heaven for the sound of your laughter. Do you think your sorrow makes him happy? He is celebrating a wonderful life with Jesus. I'm sure he misses your smile and your joking. I'm sure he wants you to be happy and he wants his child to experience the same joy you brought to him while he was here with you to share it. Please put away the self-sacrifice of mourning. Let's fill this place with joy so that Jacob's child can enter into it with us."

She smiled at him. "You've been waiting a long time to say those things to me. I was just asking God today how much longer he wanted me to be sad. I promise tomorrow I will not be wearing black or shutting myself away from you. You are right. This house needs to have some joy in it."

"Amelia, Paul did not go to that tavern expecting any of his actions would get Jacob killed. I know you want to blame someone. The man who stabbed Jacob has never been discovered, but holding this against Paul is wrong. He loved Jacob like a brother. He was always kind to both of you. Find a way to forgive him. Holding this against him is only taking a piece of your heart and making it bitter." Keith urged her.

She got up from the table before she was finished eating. "So much of this is wrong and has no reason behind it. I was married to a loving and honorable man who was just defending the honor of his sister. Does this sort of thing happen often in a tavern? Do men just jump in and fight? I play that day over and over again in my mind. I dream of Jacob walking into a knife. I wake up in the middle of the night thinking that I am covered in his blood. I have no way to peace in the darkness. There is no one to turn to when I am so frightened I can barely breathe. I hate going to bed. I stay up late to avoid the loneliness of it and the terror of my dreams. In the midst of that, you turn to me and ask me to forgive. Maybe your words are from God. Maybe forgiveness will give me peace; but if I give it, then who do I blame for his death?"

Keith listened and then he got up to go to her. "Amelia, why didn't you tell me about the nightmares?"

"What could you do?" She asked.

"I could have been available to you. I could have told you to wake me. We could have sat together until the fear left you." He said.

"Yes, that would look good among your servants. A widow loses her husband and runs for comfort into another man's room. They would view me as disgraceful." She said.

"You shut me out because of the judgment of our servants? That is needless suffering. I can arrange for them to be out of the manor at night. I can arrange anything that will help you find peace." He said.

The offer surprised her. "No servants in the manor at night? How would you manage?"

He smiled. "I would manage just fine, and you know it.

Beginning tonight, there will be no servants in the manor. I am completely available to you until these night terrors stop."

"You are very kind, Keith." She told him. "It won't be necessary. Just find a girl you can trust and have her stay up in my sitting room at night. If I need you, I will send her to wake you."

"I promise you, I will always be available to you." He said.

"Can we take a ride to see Paul and Olivia? I need to speak with them, and I am missing Olivia very much." She told him.

"I will arrange it for tomorrow afternoon." He agreed.

That evening he introduced her to Beth. "She will come to get me if you need me."

"She is so young." Amelia remarked.

"I am a man, Amelia. Beth is too young for me to consider and I like it that way. Besides, little girls run faster than older women." He explained. Then he addressed Beth. "You will come to me if you hear Miss Amelia scream or cry out. You will not wait for her to tell you to come. You will run as fast as you can to my door and knock on it. Do not enter. Yell to me from the hall. Do you understand?"

"Yes, Lord Chalon." She answered.

"You will wait for my order when I come out of my room." Keith told her.

"Yes, Lord Chalon." She answered.

That evening Beth proved her value. As Amelia tossed and

cried out in her sleep, Beth overheard her and ran directly to Keith. She banged on his bedroom door. "Lord Chalon, there is trouble with Miss Amelia."

Keith was quick to get up. "Go to bed now, Beth." He told her as he came out of his room. He hurried to Amelia's room and could hear the torment she was suffering as he stood outside her door. He let himself in and went to her. "Amelia." He whispered.

She woke up immediately and hugged him around the neck.

He held on to her. "It was just a dream, Amelia. You are safe."

She yelled in pain and grabbed her side.

"What is wrong? Are you still dreaming?" He asked her.

"No, it's the baby. I need the midwife." She told him.

Keith got right up. "Is the baby early?"

"No, the baby is not early. Keith, please get the midwife."

He left the room and came back a few minutes later. "She is coming. What can I do for you?"

Amelia smiled. "Nothing but wait."

"Alright." He sat in the chair by the bed.

"You do know you will have to leave while I do this?" She asked.

"Oh yes. I wasn't going to stay. I am just waiting for the midwife. I don't want to leave you alone until she gets here."

He said.

A few minutes later the midwife came. "Lord Chalon, it is time for you to leave."

"Yes, of course." He kissed Amelia on the forehead. "I will be waiting. If you need anything send someone to me with the request. I will honor whatever you request of me."

"Go back to bed, Keith. It is the middle of the night and this will take a long time." She told him.

"No, Amelia. I will wait." He said.

"You said you would honor any request I made. My request is that you go back to your room, climb into your bed and sleep. Check on me in the morning." She said.

"You have trapped me by my own word. I will honor your request." He agreed. He turned to the midwife. "Be careful of her and the baby. Send someone for me if you need me. I want someone to wake me as soon as the baby is here."

"Yes, Lord Chalon." The midwife agreed as she escorted him to the door.

He left and went back to bed. He had trouble falling asleep, but eventually he did. In the morning, he got dressed and asked one of the older women he employed to go check on Amelia. She came back to him a few minutes later.

"Miss Amelia is very tired but the baby is expected soon." She told him.

Keith had his breakfast, and then he walked into Amelia's section of the house. He was surprised when he heard her screaming out in pain. He knocked on her bedroom door and one of the ladies who was helping the midwife stepped out of the room to talk to him.

"Why is she screaming? Are you causing her pain?" He asked.

The woman was startled by the question. "No, Lord Chalon. The baby is causing her the pain. There is nothing we can do about that. Every woman screams."

"Like that?" He was surprised.

"Yes, just like that." She answered.

"Let me know when the baby comes. I will be in my office." He walked away quickly and went to the room furthest away from Amelia's room.

About an hour later, one of the servants came to get him. "Lady Amelia has a baby boy. She will see you now."

Keith got right up and went to her.

She was leaning against her pillows holding her son in her arms when he entered. She reached her hand out to Keith and he took it. "Look at him. He looks so much like Jacob."

Keith sat on the bed next to her. "You look beautiful and tired." He said to her as he felt the baby's fingers.

"I am going to name him Jacob after his father." Amelia decided.

"I think Jacob would have wanted that. It is a perfect name for a perfect baby boy." Keith agreed.

"Keith, I want to talk to you alone." She requested.

He turned and motioned for everyone to leave. When the door shut as the last one left, he told her, "Ask anything of me and I will grant it."

"I ask for the absolute truth to this important question." She said.

He smiled. "You shall have it. What is your question?"

"Do you love me?" She asked.

"I just want to be clear what you are asking." He replied.

"Keith, do you love me like a dear sister or like someone you might want to marry?" She asked.

"Well, that is specific. I promised you the truth and I will speak it. Amelia, I have loved you since the day you tackled my brother in the hall with kisses. I grew more in love with you the day you slipped him those large panties and claimed they were your own. I loved you every moment of every day, but I kept that love in my heart because Jacob was the one you loved. I understood your commitment to him and his to you. I respected your marriage. I wanted my brother to cherish you forever. I would have never told you of my love if he had lived to grow old with you. I pictured myself settling for second best and being content with it. I do love you with all that I am and all that I have. If you never love me back and wish to be with someone else, I will honor your choice and pray for your happiness. All I want for you is joy. All I want for this baby is joy. I would marry you tomorrow if you would have me, but I will never bring it up again. I don't want you to consider it out of obligation or pressure. When you are sure of it, you tell me." He answered.

"Keith, marry me. I want to have a good father for my son, and I can think of no better man." She said.

"Amelia, don't settle for me because of the baby. When we wed, if we wed, I want all of you. I don't want a mother to the child I love. I want a wife to hold and to kiss and to make love to. I want a partner to help me run things. I will raise Jacob and hug him and teach him without having to be married to you. Don't settle for me, Amelia. When you want me as your husband in every sense because you love me, then tell me and I will marry you in a moment." He said.

"Keith, you are not like your brother in so many ways. You are so different, but so honorable. I've watched you for months. I've listened to your voice and felt your touch on my hand. You have a passion inside you that Jacob did not have. You are passionate about paintings and music. You love creativity and the things that look confusing but can be explained. You don't just want to learn French, you want to dwell in the culture and understand the why parts of it. I've noticed so much about you these many months. I will not hold myself back from you. I want to be in your arms. I need to feel love again, and I want that from you and you alone. I trust you with me." She said.

"Amelia, even yesterday you cried for Jacob. He is still part of who you are." He said.

"I will still cry for Jacob no matter when and who I would choose to marry. He is missing time with his own son. I cry because his death makes no sense to me. It will never make sense. Those feelings need to be understood not feared. You mourn your brother too. I've seen you cry for him when you hide away in the garden. Give us this chance to heal our hearts together. You say you love me. I'm asking you to trust me. Marry me, and stop asking yourself so many questions about it." She told him.

He leaned toward her and kissed her on the lips. "I refuse to feel like I am betraying Jacob by kissing you. I have no guilt or shame about how I feel about you or what I want."

"He would approve now. He understands the circumstances." She touched his face, and he knew she wanted him to kiss her again.

He kissed the palm of her hand and then her lips. "When you are well, we will have the minister marry us."

"When I am well, we will celebrate our marriage with our friends and your family. I want witnesses to my new happiness. I will not be married in silence as if I am ashamed of my choice." She insisted.

He smiled. "We will do it exactly the way you want it done."

"Keith, please ask Olivia and Paul to come to see me and the baby. Let them know that I want them both here. It is time to forgive and ask for forgiveness. Also, I want Charles and Yvette to come and see the baby. We haven't had them here to visit since I moved in. I want to fill the house with our family. I want to have dinner parties and celebrate life again."

Keith asked if he could hold the baby. Amelia handed Jacob to him. He cradled the child in his arms.

"You have transformed our lives this day. I hope you realize that the blessing of God is upon you. Your father will love you from heaven all your life, but I will be your father while you are here with us. When you are older I will tell you wonderful things that you don't know about him. I will tell you what a privilege it was to have known him. I promise that to you." Then Keith looked up toward heaven. "Jacob Douglas look at your little boy! He looks just like you and I will take good care of him, with his mother's help of course." Keith smiled at Amelia.

She had tears in her eyes. "You touch my heart, Keith Chalon."

"I plan on doing that each day. Amelia, name him Jacob Douglas Chalon. I want him to belong to the three of us." He handed the baby to her. "He looks hungry. I will leave you to feed him. I will send a servant to you. You make sure to rest after you feed him. I will come to check on you both later. If you need me send someone to get me." He kissed her on the cheek and left the room.

"Come now, little one, let us figure this out together." Amelia said as she positioned him to nurse. "Your name shall be Jacob Douglas Chalon."

Keith went out and found Madeline. She had helped Amelia with the birth that morning. "Madeline, you will give Lady Amelia a few minutes with her son alone. Then if she will let you, take the child and care for him personally so that she can sleep. Wake her only if the baby needs her. I want you available to her during the day. When you have to leave to eat or for any other important matter, have Beth stay with her and watch over the baby. I will send Beth to you in a few hours."

"Yes, Lord Chalon." She answered.

"Madeline, I understand the protocols of titles very well. Normally you would refer to my guest as Miss Amelia; however, if you work for me, you shall refer to her as Lady Amelia from now on."

"Yes, Lord Chalon." She answered.

A few hours later Keith knocked lightly on Amelia's door. Madeline let him into the room.

"She and the baby are both asleep. He is beautiful." She walked with him to Jacob's cradle.

Keith smiled. "You may leave for an hour. I will stay with them. Have Beth stay in the sitting room. I will send her for you if I need you." He whispered.

"Yes, Lord Chalon." Madeline left the room.

Amelia woke up about thirty minutes later and saw him sitting in the chair. "How long have you been watching me sleep?" She whispered.

He came to sit on the bed next to her. "Not long. You still look tired."

"I am still tired. I had a dream about Jacob. It was the first good dream I've had since he died. He came to me and kissed me on the lips. He told me I was beautiful. Then he walked to the cradle and looked at his son. Suddenly he had angels' wings. They were magnificent, pure white with lights of many colors like they were sparkling in the sun. Then he saw you enter the room and he smiled." She told him.

"That sounds like it could have happened." Keith said.

"Yes, it does. For the first time in a long time I feel such peace. Everything in my heart is well. How wonderful for God to allow me to have a dream like that. I shall never forget it." She said.

"You should write it down and keep it for Jacob. He would want to know about such a dream." Keith told her.

"I will do that." She agreed. "Keith, I will need Madeline now. Can you find her?"

"I will send Beth to bring her back to you." He got up from the bed and went to the door. He gave orders to Beth and watched her run to find Madeline. "She should be here soon. Are you alright?" He went back to the bed.

"I think so. I am just uncomfortable and sore. You will need to leave when she gets here. I am going to try to sleep a little more after she attends me."

"That is fine. I will check on you later." He waited. When Madeline came into the room, he left.

Chapter Fifteen

Two weeks later Paul and Olivia came as invited guests to see the baby. Olivia enjoyed holding Jacob. Paul complimented the baby and congratulated Amelia.

"Duke Chalon, may I speak with you alone?" Amelia asked.

Paul stepped out of the room with her. "What is it, Amelia?"

"You know that I blamed you for Jacob's death. That is why I came here to live in Lord Chalon's manor." She said.

"Yes, I am aware of how you feel about me. I am truly sorry about Jacob's death." He told her.

"I know that now. His death did not make sense to me. It will never make sense to me. In my grief, I wanted someone to be responsible for it. You seemed the logical choice at the time. I'm sorry for putting the blame on you. You did not go to the tavern that day and plan the death of someone you loved and cared about. It was ridiculous for me to blame you. What happened just happened, and we cannot change the result of it. Please forgive me for adding to your sorrow." She said.

"I understand, Amelia. There is nothing to forgive. We all suffered because of Jacob's death. I certainly did not want to lose you both from my household. Would you consider coming back and helping Olivia? She is lost without you as a translator. My mother has been trying to teach her French but it is a slow process. We could provide someone to watch the baby when you are needed." He said.

"I do not think my future husband would approve of that." She smiled.

"You mean Keith?" He was surprised.

"Yes. We planned on telling everyone today." She said.

"I'm sure the rest of them will be as surprised as I am." Paul was happy for her.

"I hope it is a good surprise." Amelia crossed her fingers.

"None of that Amelia. It will be a good surprise. Keith is a very nice man, and you are a very nice woman. That baby will need you both." Paul said.

"Let's go back to Olivia and Keith." Amelia opened the door to the sitting room. Then she joined Keith by standing next to him. She whispered. "Duke Chalon knows of our plan to marry."

"Olivia, we have an announcement to make." Keith said.

I looked up at them and waited.

"Amelia and I are getting married soon." Keith announced.

"You are? Why?" I am sure they saw the obvious shock on my face.

"Because we love each other and Jacob needs loving parents to raise him." Keith answered.

"I'm stunned that you would consider this. Jacob has not been gone a year and Keith, you are his brother." I reminded them.

Keith was about to be upset with me, but Amelia stopped him. She came to sit next to me while I held the baby in my arms.

"Duchess, do you believe there is a heaven?" She asked.

"Yes, of course." I replied.

"Do you believe it is a beautiful place full of joy and the loving presence of God?" Amelia asked.

"Yes." I answered.

"Do you believe Jacob is there?" She asked.

"Absolutely." I said.

"My husband left me and went to heaven. He is surrounded by goodness, love, joy and beauty. He talks to Jesus each day and walks among angels. There is no sorrow for him there. He spends his time celebrating with others who have been blessed and accepted by God. I am left here to care for his son. It does not matter if he has been gone a week or a year. The fact is that I am here without his love. Do you want me to force myself away from a man who could love me completely just because Jacob's memory has not cost me enough sorrow? Am I not entitled to love someone and be in love? Isn't my son entitled to have a father here in this place to love him from the beginning of his birth? Keith is an extraordinary man. He has supported me and comforted me. He never demanded my affection. He gave me time to observe him. I became captivated by his love for me. I asked him to marry me, and he said yes. I wanted him as much as he wanted me. That is a rare gift to happen twice in a person's life. Do you want me to pretend to mourn while Jacob is in heaven celebrating his new life there? Do you want me to convince you that I miss him beyond words? Haven't I convinced you already? Should I make you feel better by denying my love for Keith? Olivia, you were blessed to live with three wonderful men growing up. I am blessed that two of them chose to love me. I lost one already. I won't lose another." Amelia said.

"I'm sorry, Amelia. Traditions have blurred my vision. I can see that Keith loves you, and it is obvious you love him. I would not wish you to lose love again. These are odd circumstances indeed; then again, my family has lived through an abundance of odd circumstances. When you plan your wedding, please include us as your guests." I told them.

Yvette and Charles joined us in the sitting room. Yvette was thrilled to hold the baby in her arms.

"Charles, we need to get on this. I want many children." She said enthusiastically.

He laughed. "Yes, Dear. How soon do you want one of those?"

"Nine months." She answered seriously and we all laughed.

We were having a wonderful time together when Keith told Yvette and Charles that he was going to marry Amelia.

Charles shook his hand immediately. "I'm sure you two will be very happy together. Little Jacob has certainly struck gold with you two as his parents."

I was surprised by Charles' enthusiasm. He took me aside later.

"Olivia, I'm not shocked they are getting married. Keith adores Amelia and Jacob wouldn't have wanted her to be alone, especially with a son. Who better to teach him how to hunt and fish than Keith? Keith has more skills than Jacob or I ever had. That child is blessed to have him take over for the father he lost. Be happy for them, Olivia. God's perfect plan is still working everything out. We keep Amelia in the family and Keith happy with our approval. It is a win-win situation." Charles told me.

"How about you, Charles? Are you happy?" I asked him.

"Yes. I would advise any man to marry a plain woman. Yvette's personality is multifaceted. She is delightful and adventurous. She continually surprises me in so many ways. I will never be bored with that woman. She has such inner beauty I feel like I have been given a gift each day. I cannot describe to you how amazing my life is with her in it. I hate myself for referring to her as plain, because she really isn't. To me she is stunningly beautiful. She turns her head or brushes out her hair and I am mad for her. She scrunches up her face and I laugh with delight. I am very happy. I want that kind of happiness for you and for Keith."

I hugged him. "You are continually the wonderful older brother. Thank you, Charles."

"You are quite welcome. Let's go join the others. I can tell Amelia and Yvette are entertaining everyone. We are missing all the laughter." He said as we walked back toward the sitting room.

The day was filled with joy and hope - something all of us needed in our lives since Jacob died. I was happy for my brothers and the women they loved.

"What are you looking at, Olivia?" Paul asked me as he came to stand behind me at the window as I looked out that evening.

"Jacob's grave. I know he's not there. At least the conversation I had with Amelia today put that in perspective. She is right. He is in heaven enjoying the pleasures of being within an arm's reach of God. How wonderful that must be." I moved my head to kiss him on the cheek.

"You seem better today. Actually, everyone seemed better." He said as he moved my nightgown off my shoulders and kissed my neck.

I turned around. "I love you, Paul."

He put his arms around me with my big belly in the way. "We were blessed to find each other and blessed to keep each other. I don't take any of that for granted Olivia."

"I know. You've changed so much for the better. Even the servants like you more now. You have made quite an impression." I told him.

He kissed me and moved me toward our bed. "Right now, Duchess, the only one I care about impressing is you."

He laid me on the bed gently and my water broke.

"What just happened?" He asked.

"The baby doesn't want you to impress me tonight." I smiled. "Go get the midwife."

Chapter Sixteen

As Paul rushed to get dressed and ran out of the bedroom, I had to laugh. There he was, the grand Duke Chalon, frantic about having a baby. It was me who was destined to do all the work. Early the next day, I gave birth to our first child, a boy. We named him Daniel. He was thoroughly spoiled until his sister was born two years later. She conquered the name Quinn, notably a boy's name by tradition, but we were wise in our choice. She grew to be independent and a challenge for her father. Then came Robert, Jade, and Michael our youngest.

Charles and Yvette had all girls. He was a good Papa to each of them. They were real beauties, not a plain one among the seven of them. This drove Charles a bit crazy. I think his years of training having to protect me from men paid off when his girls came of age.

Keith and Amelia had another boy and two girls. They continued to love each other beyond measure. Their children enjoyed their parents' sense of humor. They grew to be fine men and women.

Jacob was told many wonderful things about his father, Jacob. He appreciated the stories, but it was Keith whom he loved and was devoted to. Jacob was part of a complete family. He was never treated differently or viewed differently.

It was the finest living testimony to our family as a whole.

I've changed over the years. I'm not as innocent and naïve as I once was. Life does that to each of us. Sometimes people hold on to God so tightly during the roughest times in their lives, and then, when it is good they start to relax their grip. They put His word away to gather dust on a shelf. I have found that if I am consistently filled with His word and His presence, there is no battle I cannot win by faith and in prayer.

God Bless,

Olivia Adriana Chalon

Olivia's Story

For those who feel like they have been in a dry well. You want to seek God, but life has gotten in the way too often. Read this each day and let this Word of God by its own power change your life.

Psalm 63 (N.I.V.)

O God, you are my God, earnestly I seek you; my soul thirsts for you, my body longs for you, in a dry and weary land where there is no water.

I have seen you in the sanctuary and beheld your power and your glory.

Because your love is better than life, my lips will glorify you.

I will praise you as long as I live, and in your name I will lift up my hands.

My soul will be satisfied as with the richest of foods, with singing lips my mouth will praise you.

On my bed I remember you; I think of you through the watches of the night.

Because you are my help, I sing in the shadow of your wings.

My soul clings to you; your right hand upholds me.

They who seek my life will be destroyed; they will go down to the depths of the earth.

They will be given over to the sword and become food for the jackals.

But the king will rejoice in God; all who swear by God's name will praise him, while the mouths of liars will be silenced.

Olivia's Story

Made in the USA
Middletown, DE
10 February 2022